A
John Quinton Cord
Novel

Tiger's Code

Betty J. Vaughn

TotalRecall Publications, Inc.
1103 Middlecreek
Friendswood, Texas 77546
281-992-3131 TEL
www.totalrecallpress.com

ISBN: ISBN: 978-1-59095-391-4
UPC: 6-43977-43916-1

Library of Congress Control Number: 2017949347

Printed in the United States of America with simultaneous
printings in Australia, Canada, and United Kingdom.

FIRST EDITION
1   2   3   4   5   6   7   8   9   10

My heartfelt thanks to my love James M. Atwater for his support, encouragement, and wise suggestions. Thanks also to Colonel Jim Braddock, for reading and commenting on the initial chapters. And for her continuing love, my gratitude to my daughter Joanna Elisabeth Meredith.

About the Author

Betty J. Vaughn has written all of her life, winning awards in school and afterwards. Following a career teaching AP art history and painting, she wrote her first novel, Yesterday's Magnolia, quickly followed by four historical novels. The Man in the Chimney; Turbulent Waters; Run, Cissy, Run, and The Intrepid Miss LaRoque. The four novels in the historical series were all winners of the award for historical fiction from the NC Society of Historians. The latest novel, Tiger's Code, deals with concerns that currently plague our Nation as well as many others. A graduate of East Carolina University and a prize winning watercolorist, Mrs. Vaughn is a resident of Raleigh, NC, enjoys traveling, gardening, gourmet cooking, and reading. She is currently researching for her next book.

"Mrs. Vaughn can consider herself a seasoned novelist. Her books are fast paced, action packed, and full of adventure. Her work isn't just a flurry of words, dry and boring. She is a master of literary technique as she weaves together a tapestry of words."

About the Book

Quint Cord is an unlikely spy. With sufficient family money so that he never needs to work, he could have spent his life idling on a beach chasing women. But from the moment he discovers famous codes of the past in a university class, he is hooked. His unique talent for creating and breaking codes brings him to the attention of the CIA.

A powerful and ambitious politician, who's in cahoots with a Saudi prince, plans to seize the US presidency and throw the western world into turmoil. Quint flees the country only to stay one step ahead of a foe determined to kill him before he can break the code.

Clue by clue, Quint begins to zero in on his target but can he stop him in time?

Chapter 1

The man known only as Nemesis picked up the phone he used for business. The voice on the other end he had heard before. It was soft and muffled, disguised in some way. It didn't matter to Nemesis who it was as long as he was paid for his work, work that he excelled in.

"I have a job for you. The usual fee. There can be no mistakes."

"I understand. Have I made mistakes before?" The hand holding the phone tightened in anger.

"If you had, you would know it." The man's voice was cold when he said it. Nemesis didn't need a translator to figure out that message.

He snarled, "The particulars only. I don't need your threats."

"I don't threaten. I just don't believe in loose ends and wasted money." The man went on to provide the name and details of the target.

Nemesis hung up his phone and sat in contemplation. One day he would take out the son of a bitch that had just hired him. The arrogant fool should know better than to threaten him no matter how veiled he did so.

*****

John Quinton Cord, whose father had cursed him with the nickname "Sissy Quincey," flipped the pages of the Julia Child cookbook to continue the recipe for Coq au Vin. Turning back to the chicken that lay on a disposable sheet on his immaculate countertop, he continued the prep. Laying his knife to one side of the sheet, he carefully smoothed his right glove back in place. Quinton had an aversion to touching raw flesh. Under the counter were two new boxes of latex gloves as he had a horror of running out. He didn't even want to think about the reasons. Too block the thought, he allowed the strains of Marcello's Concerto per Oboe in D Minore to wash over him before he resumed cutting up the chicken.

His dog Code looked up at him from his station at the end of the counter. Quint laughed, "You hungry, too, boy?"

Code was his friend...had been the only one for a long time. He couldn't afford friends in his business. Friendships require intimacy and he was in no position to offer it. As an expert at encryptions and an international spy, he kept to himself to avoid emotional entanglements that could cloud his judgment. Lapses in judgment were a quick method for finding oneself in a starring role in the cemetery. He liked his life too much for that. With Code as confidant, his music, and Julia Child for inspiration, he was content, even if at times he wondered if there might be something more for him. Quint whistled to the music to take his mind off his new assignment. He had tried to decline, as he did not like leaving Code for as long as would be required. In the end, he had been given no choice. He had known he wouldn't be allowed to refuse when he objected.

He was 32 years old and at times he tired of living in the shadows of the night like some non-existent entity. He was wealthy enough that he never needed to work, thanks to very generous trusts established for him in infancy. He worked because it amused him. He had become enmeshed in government intrigue because of his reputation for cracking the toughest of codes and writing even tougher ones. He relished that reputation. He had earned it by cracking a code that led to the foiling of a Taliban attack on the U.S. Embassy in Amman, Jordan. The head of CIA was impressed enough to hire him on contract and had used him several times for code breaking. Soon he was sent on location to various European cities. His language skills and ability to blend in allowed him to get closer to the source of some of the codes that were of increasing concern to the CIA, especially after the rise of more militant factions in the Muslim brotherhood. On those assignments, he was essentially operating as a spy with very specific goals.

Catching his image reflected in the long window by the kitchen door, he studied himself. He wasn't handsome. He wasn't ugly. Not tall, nor short, not fat, nor skinny. He decided the best description was non-descript. He would have liked to have been a better-looking fellow, maybe chase women who would naturally fall at his debonair feet. But nature had not intended that. His looks were a blessing though for the role in which he now found himself. It was good that he was a loner, someone who lived in his head. Otherwise it would have been a miserable life. Squelching that line of thought, he reminded himself he was content with his lot. He took pride in his work, work that none other yet equaled. Raised as the son of a patriot, that part of his patrimony had taken. He was proud to be doing something to help his country in a perilous time.

While the chicken was cooking, he scoured the work surface with disinfectant, wiping down the faucet as well, before stripping off the gloves. That done he walked over to his wine rack and pulled out a nice Russian River pinot noir. Most of his table wines were from that area of California. His better California and European wines he kept in the wine cellar below the kitchen. Bottles of wine costing well into the hundreds were not something one would expect to see in a modest house with Rooms-to-Go furnishings.

The wine cellar was Quint's own design, accessed through the secret door in the back of the broom closet. The door was solid steel and only his left thumbprint followed by his right index finger print opened the high-tech locks that held it secure. Both the locks and the steel door were hidden behind a trip-sprung wooden panel that matched the sidewalls of the closet. An identical access point was cleverly hidden in his bedroom closet. He had installed that, too. Narrow stairways led from the two steel doors into the basement. From both sets of stairs a hidden door led into narrow corridors leading to a workroom, as well as directly into the wine cellar. Once there, it looked like nothing more than a wine cellar. But, there was far more than that. Cleverly concealed was his fire and bombproof office with backup generator, and an escape hatch should the need arise. The Office with the escape hatch access was hidden behind a wall paneled with the ends of wine boxes. A simple trigger hidden in the edge of one of the boxes caused a section of the panels to swing out allowing access to the secret room. Both of the entry doors into the wine cellar were cleverly concealed on the adjacent wall using the same decor. However, the triggers for opening those doors were hidden in the tile flooring. Only by stepping on a separate and correct sequence of tiles would each of them open to allow exit from the cellar. From the secret workshop area, a hidden cement lined tunnel ran to a large bush near the street where he could pop up like a gopher from his hole. Branching off from the main tunnel, another tunnel led to his garage where a car waited, full of gas, weapons, cash, untraceable spare phones that he kept fully charged, a wallet containing four alias passports with credit cards under each name, and two packed suitcases filled with clothing appropriate for either warm or cold weather. No one could tell by looking, but half of the back wall of the garage was rigged to slide up so if anyone were watching the front of the house, they would not see him leave. He had carefully planted concealing bushes on either side allowing him to drive off onto the back street undetected from the front. His escape car was registered under an alias; the other car in the garage was under his own name.

When he first started in his line of work, he blithely assumed he was safe and obscure enough no one would come for him. Narrowly escaping with his life when a foreign government sent an agent to take him out, he had made carefully thought out changes. Buying the house and then adapting it to his needs was the first. Next, he planted weapons and tripwires. Then he began a regimen of exercises to increase agility and sharpen his reflexes. Lessons in mixed marshal arts gave him a range of defensive and offensive maneuvers. A five-mile run every morning had given him stamina. Through practice and native acumen, he became an expert marksman. He might look harmless but he was far from it. Quint was taking no chances on another near miss.

The bell on his timer dinged reminding him to take the loaf of yeast bread from the oven. While it was cooling he quickly made a mesculan salad and dressed it with his special vinaigrette. With the coq au vin ready to serve, the wine breathing in a carafe... and the table covered with a crisp linen tablecloth and set with, china, crystal, silver and monogrammed napkins from his mother, and a lit candelabra...he was almost ready. All that remained was to switch the music to some Chopin and slice the bread. He carried everything into the dining room and seated himself. His mother, who refused to call him John or Jack and had always called him Quinton, would be proud that he maintained the style of dining that she had insisted on in her home. His father, who was usually away on a business trip to some site in his far-flung commercial empire, rarely noticed the table or what he was eating. Both long dead now, it was his mother that he missed most. Silently he raised his glass in a toast to the portrait of his mother that hung on the wall at the far end of his table.

At his right, he kept a note pad for jotting down ideas for codes he wanted to write, or for solving ones that he had been tasked with. As he ate, he reflected on the latest assignment, one that would take him to London and perhaps Paris or beyond. Working with Interpol and the CIA, he was to decode intercepted transmissions between terrorist cells in Washington, Paris and another operating out of London. While the investigating agencies managed to crack into the communication stream, it did them no good as they could not decipher the code in which the messages were written. They expected him to accomplish what others had failed to do. The Agency did not know it, but using the information they had given him he did not need to go through them to hack into future transmissions.

When he first began working on a code he just lived with it, trying to absorb the pattern, the rhythm of it. Some were simple letter-number substitutions and the pattern easy to discern.

Others were far more complex with no apparent pattern. This was one of those. He continuously glanced at the code that he had scribbled on his pad. If he waited, it would soon begin to speak to him. It was almost mystical, he decided, to just open your mind and wait for inspiration.

Quint was nervous that night, and sleep elusive. He had learned to trust his gut, but at the moment he could not figure out what it was trying to tell him. He just knew that something seemed off. Going over the last few days in his mind, he tried to remember anything that might have caused the unease but nothing stood out as significant. He was glad when dawn came. Wasting no time, he made coffee and drank it while glancing at the headlines in the News and Observer. That done he cleaned up before putting on his running shoes. The early morning run helped him think and it usually settled his nerves.

Code was standing at the door waiting for him, his leash in his mouth. Snapping it into place, Quint patted the dog's head. "You ready to go meet your girlfriends, boy?"

Code woofed, and wagged his tail as if in agreement causing Quint to chuckle at his dog's eager expression.

Setting the trip wires and the alarm, he left his house and jogged down Park Street toward Pullen Park in a neighborhood that was rapidly gentrifying. He had chosen the area as it was close to the university and the sophisticated computer geeks there, and because the houses were lower middleclass and not ones to draw attention. While Raleigh might seem a bit remote from his bosses in Arlington, he liked it that way. With direct air connections to Washington and other major cities in the country and to London and Paris, as well, it was a convenient location. Not only that, but he had maintained his parents' home on the coast for weekends away. The cottage was only a couple of hours drive from his house.

Quint and Code crossed the street and entered the park. He had just rounded the last stretch of his run when he felt a percussion of air at his ear followed by the thud of a bullet slamming into the tree to his right. Code barked and knocked him to the ground. Both he and the dog rolled under the thick shrubbery just off the path. Another bullet, followed by two more, kicked dirt at his feet. Whoever the asshole was, he was bent on murder and had come prepared. Quint could tell the weapon the man was using was a high-powered rifle with a silencer attached. His heart hammering, he reached for his pistol, cursing when he did not find it in his pocket. Of all the mornings to leave it at home, he would have picked this one. Crouching into a run, he and Code moved into thicker brush.

It was all he could do to restrain his dog from going after the shooter. Quint wasn't about to let his dog go, just to have some SOB shoot him. Dashing from bush to bush, Quint kept a wary eye out for the shooter who had not fired again. Judging from the trajectory of the bullet and the possible range of the weapon, he couldn't tell if he was close or some distance away. On the university campus the bell tower poked out above the trees. Was that movement in the tower? Or was the assassin on the roof of one of the nearby buildings. While he couldn't be sure, it was no time to take chances no matter the location. He figured there was no choice except to stay down and out of sight until the shooter moved on.

"Sit, Code, and be quiet. Whoever that is wants us dead and I don't care to oblige him."

Code growled low in his throat as Quint pushed him further back.

"Calm down boy. We're going to hunker down here twenty minutes or so. If nothing else happens, we're going home as carefully as we can." Quint brushed a spider off his sleeve and snuggled further into the large azalea bush, effectively hiding them both from view. As he sat there listening, he couldn't help but question his sanity. Here he sat, the target in a turkey shoot, cramped and irritated by the branches that kept poking him every time he turned his head when he could be sunning on a beach along the Riviera, a drink in one hand and a woman in the either. The thought caused him to grin. His work was dangerous, but it for damned sure never bored him. He would think about retiring to the beach when he was older, if he made it that long.

It puzzled him that someone would be trying to take him out. The last time that happened the hired killer had been arrested and the source of the hire identified. Since then he had been involved in nothing that would warrant someone trying to kill him. The latest assignment was too new for someone to already be after him in connection with it, wasn't it? The only ones that should know of the assignment were his contact at the CIA and whoever pulled his strings.

Pulling his phone out he dialed Uber. He was not going to risk being shot at again today. His phone pinged telling him the driver was two minutes away. Tired of the cramped position, he gladly arose and stretched his limbs. "Let's get moving, Code. A car is on the way."

Quint wasted no time settling Code with his basket of toys in the secure room in the basement. Logging onto his computer, he quickly typed in the access code that would take him directly to his contact in the CIA, a man he referred to by the designated alias 'G'. He thought for a moment before he began to type. He had to let the Agency know that he had been attacked and his identity compromised. He hoped that they would take the assignment from him and give it to someone else. He could always continue on his own to solve the code. He was enjoying the challenge of it too much to quit. They didn't need to know that though. He shut down his computer and secured the area before triggering the alarms. A special server would continue relaying photos of his property inside and out along with other info he had programmed into it. He had forty-five seconds to exit the basement and another forty-five to exit the garage. If someone triggered the alarm, the upstairs of his house would go up like carnival fireworks gone bad.

That done, he walked over to his dog and said, "Let's go, Code. We're getting the hell out of here until things cool down."

Quint triggered the access to the tunnel and wasted no time getting both of them into his car in the garage. Using the special remote, he raised the rear wall and drove off as it slid home on silent rollers. In two hours he would be at the cottage. After he began working for the CIA, he had sold the cottage to a Jefferson Quarls, a neat alias he thought. He did not want it to be tied to him if anyone went searching. He then made the same alterations for security there that he had in the house in Raleigh. Not even the Agency was aware of his bolthole. When he reached Interstate 440, he rolled down his window and tossed the latest cell phone from the window. If someone were tracking him on it, they would be out of luck.

The shooter sat in his car down the block from Quint's house keeping watch. He had been there since the abortive mission that morning. When the target left the house he intended to assure he would not be returning. He swore to himself. If it had not been for the fucking pigeon landing beside him in the tower and throwing off his aim, he would not be sitting in a damned rental car with an overwhelming urge to piss. Sometimes he wished he had continued in the FBI. He shifted on his seat to relieve his bladder. There should have been lights or some kind of activity in the house even if his target were not going out. He would give it another hour and then he was going in. His designated wait was nearly up when his phone rang.

He knew who it was before he answered. "I'm on it. You didn't give me a timeline so just sit tight."

"He's done a runner. I don't know where he went, but I'll let you know as soon as he checks in with the CIA."

Chapter 2

Quint snuggled into the sheets in the bed he had slept in since childhood. Moonlight shone through the large window beside his bed. He had raised it to listen to the surf. He could not image anything more lulling or peaceful. Turning on his right side, he looked through the window at the gleaming white sand that lined the beach in front of his house, bright even at night...especially when like tonight the moon was full. He could almost feel his mother nearby whispering 'goodnight' in a voice as soft as the night breeze. Reaching out he patted Code's head, "It feels good to be home again, boy."

He was glad he had kept the cottage, a mansion really with views towards the inlet to the south and the ocean straight in front. While it had been a second home prior to his parent's retirement, it became the primary residence in their final years. He felt secure with his alias and the precautions he had taken. Not only that, but exclusive Figure Eight Island could be reached by one of three ways: over a gated bridge, by water, or from the air. Unless it were a sea plane, arrival by air was unlikely and too obvious. With that thought in mind, he plumped his pillow and fell into deep sleep.

Code slept as well, waking periodically to check that all was quiet before putting his head back down to dream of chasing rabbits. He was protective of his master. A trained police dog, the German Shepherd was as cautious as Quint.

After a run on the beach and a breakfast of bacon and eggs for both of them, courtesy of Mattie Henderson the long-time housekeeper. Quint turned on his computer in the office downstairs. Using the Tor system with the new Onion Routing for anonymity, he went through a circuitous series of links that circled the globe, all non-traceable, before logging onto the Agency and his contact.

"*Quint. Where are you man?*"

"*I'm fine. Out of town. Don't worry about it.*" He didn't intend to tell anyone where he was until he knew why someone was out to kill him. "*Did you get me off this last case, or not?*"

"*Sorry, man. No can do. We need your expertise on this one. They aren't willing to consider anyone else...don't think anyone else can do it.*"

"*Really?*" Quint could not help the sarcasm. "*I'm sure they tried, too.*"

"*Ah, don't get your drawers in a wad. Be flattered.*"

"*Right...*"

"*Hey, don't log off. Tell me where you are and I'll see if I can get you some protection, alright?*"

He didn't bother to answer as he softly clicked off his screen. Until he knew the killer and who had hired him, he could trust no one.

Leaning back in his chair, he propped his feet on the well-polished old desk that had belonged to his father and grandfather before him and reviewed the particulars of the case he had been assigned. The message they expected him to crack taunted him. He picked up his pad and studied it. It wasn't a code he had seen before. All he needed to do was figure out the key and it was his to read. And that was the catch...finding the key. He laid it to one side. He could wait.

The priority at the moment was staying alive and one jump

ahead of the killer and whoever had hired him. He was safe for the moment, but long term, who knew? The Agency possessed sophisticated tracking mechanisms, satellites, and he knew not what else. If the hit had been contracted through some subversive in the Agency, he was in deep shit. If the hit had been hired by a foreign entity, the Agency would be able to determine that and take action. Or so he hoped....

Walking out onto the wide veranda, Quint sat in a newly painted deck chair staring out at the ocean. He had some serious decisions to make and he didn't know how much time he had to make them. The couple that had taken care of the house for the last twenty years could be relied on to care for Code in his absence if he decided to fly to Europe and pursue the code and the authors of it. The Hendersons did not particularly care for animals and Code sensed it, but they would do it if asked. His question boiled down to whether or not he could accomplish his objective operating totally below the radar. The only way he could see that happening was to continue to intercept transmissions clandestinely. Only one person could help him with that, and she was angry with him.

Lila Carson was as beautiful and smart as they come. And expert in computer coding, he had met her when he went to North Carolina State University for help in setting up an untraceable system. Despite couching his request in other terms, she immediately saw through his obfuscation and laughed at him. Fortunately, there was something about him that she liked...a lot. They had become intermittent lovers almost immediately. Fearful of a relationship, Quint proved emotionally elusive and she was tired of being put off. The last time together, after a vigorous and very satisfying romp in the sack, she had pushed him to a commitment he knew he dared not make no matter how tempting. It was simply too dangerous for her and ultimately for him. He wanted to explain why, but the oath he had sworn to the Agency did not allow that latitude.

Taking a deep breath to gain courage, he dialed her number. She picked up on the third ring and he wasted no time saying, "Don't hang up, Lila, please. This is critically important."

"I'm sorry, do I know you?" She was being deliberately difficult.

"No, Lila, you don't, and that is where the problem lies. I wish I could explain everything but I can't. I can only ask you to please trust me and help me. I am desperate."

"How desperate?"

"Would you believe me if I told you it could make the difference between life and death?"

"Oh, come on. If you want to go to bed with me, it isn't all that dire. Just say so."

"Baby, I'd love to do just that. This isn't about our sex life. This is about trying to avoid some very nasty people."

"What in the hell have you gotten yourself into? I should have known something was up when I set up that computer chain for you." He could hear genuine concern in her voice.

"Lila, I need a big favor, please."

"Okay, okay. You know I can't say 'no" to you when you beg. What is it?"

Quint spent the next twenty minutes explaining what he needed. When he had finished, he waited for her to say something.

"I'll do it. We can keep in touch by the computer link we set up." She laughed, "So, did I just earn dinner tonight?"

"I wish I could, but I am out of town right now."

"Tomorrow then, and don't you make *me* beg."

"I truly wish I could but I may have to leave the country while I still have my skin."

"You know you frighten me sometimes."

"That's okay. I get scared as hell, too."

Quint hung up after thanking her and promising to keep in touch. He didn't deserve her but he was damned grateful he had found her. She could be relied on to be discreet and to find a way to tap into the computers he needed to monitor without either the Agency or the terrorist cells knowing he was doing it. The Agency should have known better than to leave the SOCKS notice on the messages they gave him. But then, they didn't know that he was working with a computer guru and contemplating going rogue. They thought he was just a dutiful mouse happy in his little esoteric world. He couldn't blame them. He had been for a long time. This last shooter had just stamped paid to the idea of sitting around to give the asshole another chance to kill him. Be damned if some killer was going to take him out that easily

He walked down the steps from the porch to the lower level designed with break-away walls in the event of tidal wash coming in during storms. It was there he would find Percy Henderson in the workshop he had created. Percy fancied himself a sculptor during his spare hours. He collected driftwood that he turned into imaginary creatures. Quint thought they were total tasteless kitsch, but he wasn't about to tell Percy that. Percy claimed his creatures were in high demand in local tourist shops and kept only a few for himself. All Quint asked was that Percy confine his decorating to their apartment in the attached guesthouse. The casually elegant decor his mother's interior designer had created would never be compatible with Percy's art.

"Hey, Percy. Am I interrupting?" Quint knew he was, but thought he should ask anyway.

"Well, hell yes, but what can I say? You're the boss," Percy grinned as he laid his rasp on the table. "Mama told me you got in last night. Guess I fell asleep watching television. I didn't know nothing about it until she told me this morning. You here long?"

"I wish!" Quint shook his head, "I'm probably going to clear out tonight. I wondered if you could keep an eye on Code for me for a little while?"

"Lord, I sure hope he has given up chewing on my socks. I didn't have any left after his last stay."

"I think he is past that puppy stage, but if he does any damage to your socks I'll buy you two for every pair he destroys."

"Tell Mama that. She's the one that has to clean up the mess."

"I see Code and I are going to need a serious discussion on his behavior while I'm gone. You know I would not ask you if I had anyone else I trusted."

Percy sighed, "I know. Mama and I could never say no after all you do for us. Besides, living here is like being a millionaire with all expenses paid. It's a pure paradise. I just can't see what keeps you from being here permanently."

"Believe me, there are times I ask myself the same thing."

Smelling lunch, Quint excused himself and went upstairs were he seated himself at the table overlooking the ocean. In the distance he spotted a sailboat and closer to shore dolphins capered in the breaking surf. He agreed with Percy. It was a paradise. Mattie served him a shrimp salad over crispy greens with a loaf of her crusty bread dripping with garlic butter and herbs. The aroma of yeast still hung in the air. The chilled Santa Margarita Pinto Grigio was perfect, tempting him to drink more than one glass. But he could not afford the luxury of over indulging. A slice of her strawberry pie with whipped cream topping and a cup of espresso afterwards was all he could have wanted in the way of a meal.

"Miss Mattie, I am sorry I wasn't around to marry you before Percy got the chance. He is one lucky man." Quint grinned up at her as she removed his dishes.

"Oh well, now that man of mine has some competition. I'll tell him he'd better watch out or I'll leave him for someone younger and better looking." Mattie winked at him. She laughed before turning serious, "Quinton, I don't know what you are up to, but I worry about you sometimes."

He shook his head, "No need, Mattie. I'm fine, and as long as I can come here and have you look after me when I need it, life is good."

Mattie picked up the tray of dishes and turned to go, "Whatever you are up to, be careful. We love you like a son. And with no other family for you or us, we hope you feel that way, too."

Quint jumped to his feet and swiftly walked to her and put the tray on the floor before sweeping her into a hug. "I love you, too. And thank you for everything."

He returned to his chair on the deck, crossed his hands over his satiated stomach, and studied the ever-changing sky and ocean. He pictured in his mind the steps he needed to take to avoid detection when he departed. Once he formulated a clear plan Quint left the deck and entered the garage where he removed a valise from the trunk. Taking it to his bedroom, he removed the contents. Sorting through the passport options, he selected the one he wanted and then removed a labeled plastic bag filled with the items that he would need to look like the man in the passport photo. He first dyed his hair a darker shade of brown. Since he had not shaved for two days he was beginning to grow a beard. Removing all but a nascent mustache, he then proceeded to shave off an area on the left and right sides of his hair so he would look as though he were balding at the temples. Next he picked up the glasses that would add to his disguise and settled them on his nose. A businessman's suit that allowed for extra padding around his middle came next. Code watched it all, growling low in his throat. The dog had seen the process too many times not to know that shortly he was going to be left behind.

"Hey, boy. Don't go pouting now. The Hendersons are going to feed you and take care of you. Just think, you can play in the water and chase fiddler crabs to your heart's content. You'll like it here." Quint wondered which one he was trying to console, himself or his dog? He would miss Code something fierce, but there was no way he could take him.

That completed, he repacked the items he would need for the trip. He checked his bedroom and bath to assure he was leaving nothing behind that would provide any clue that he had ever been there. As soon as he left, he knew Mattie Henderson would remake his bed and polish every surface to pristine cleanliness. It was time to go. Night had descended on the island and while he would have preferred the dark of the moon, he was not fortunate in the timing. Hugging Code goodbye, he picked up his valise and looked around the room one final time, before hurrying to the garage.

He started the car, turned off the lights, and backed out. His dog was watching from the bedroom window. He could only pray that he would be back to Code before too long. Soon he was driving off the island. He glanced in the rearview mirror watching it vanish behind him. He wondered how long it would be before he could return. Turning north onto Edgewater Club Drive and then onto Porter's Neck, Quint decided it was safe to at last turn on his lights. In a few-minutes he was driving north on Highway 17. It was the long way to go before reaching the airport he wanted, but he didn't want to take the obvious routes. The route he chose meandered through the countryside where he could stop in out of the way spots. He stopped for gas in Holly Ridge before driving on to New Bern and crossing the Neuse River. From there, he continued on through small communities, not stopping again until he saw an open Waffle House in Williamston.

Climbing from the car, he stretched and walked in. The place was empty except for the frazzled looking waitress behind the counter and an overweight cook. He sat on a stool at the bar and ordered a BLT and a coke. The waitress ignored him until time to push the bill in front of him. Her attention was on the cook, and his focused on her. Quint chuckled at their none too subtle flirtation. When he finished eating, he paid, left a tip that was adequate but not memorable and went to the toilet before once again settling behind the wheel. He wished it were daylight as the drive was a pretty one in places, going through such historic spots as Edenton and Elizabeth City before crossing the border and reaching Chesapeake and then into Norfolk.

To reach Norfolk he switched to Interstate 64, driving to the airport where he circled before driving back past the nearby Residence Inn he had spotted earlier. Just down from the motel, he backed the car into a remote space partially hidden by a large commercial dumpster. Grabbing a screwdriver, he quickly removed the license tag, set a special timer in the car, and took out his luggage. Shoving the license plate inside the dumpster beneath some particularly vile smelling garbage, he hefted his bag and walked to the hotel. Checking into reception, he booked a room for the night.

After over seven hours on the road, he was ready to sleep, but first he had to book flights and a hotel in London. Thirty minutes later he had what he needed. He would leave on the six-twenty flight for Dulles where he would have just enough time to make the flight to Heathrow. Before readying for bed, he disassembled the Heckler and Koch HK45T pistol he kept for overseas travel and scattered the parts in his hairdryer, electric razor, and other items making sure the appliances still worked afterwards. Were the electrical items checked by security and found to not work it would raise an immediate alarm.

The buzzing of his phone alarm awakened him far too early. He was still exhausted and it had been late before he could finally go to sleep. He would make up for it on the transatlantic phase of the flight. He had booked business class so he would arrive fresh and ready to execute the next phase of his plan. His plane to Dulles had cleared the ground and they were serving drinks when Quint glanced down at his watch. No doubt the fire department was busy putting out the blaze caused by the incendiary bomb he left in his car. He was leaving nothing to chance. Even the identifying numbers long since had been filed off to further assure that the car would be untraceable should he ever have to ditch it. Hopefully the carefully selected debris he left near the old Ford would be enough for the cops to pin the fire on miscreant kids and look no further for cause.

Quint allowed himself a glass of the reasonably good red wine the stewardess offered to go with the steak he selected for his dinner. Afterwards he walked to the toilet, brushed his teeth, and returned to his seat. Fortunate not to have anyone in the next seat, he was happy to avoid conversation, put his seat back and wait for sleep to claim him. When the pilot announced landing, Quint sat up and glanced at his watch. The plane should be at the gate right on schedule. By the time he went through passport control, collected his luggage and hailed a taxi, it was well after ten.

He had slept on the plane but was still tired from the adrenalin that had fired through his system since the near miss in the park. Despising the necessity, he ordered the taxi driver to drop him off at the Ritz. He waited for the cab to leave before hailing another to take him to the Millennium Hotel in Mayfair where he had booked a room. He wasted no time in checking in and going to his suite. He had taken a suite because he intended to be comfortable in what could well be his home away from home for many weeks to come. The Millennium was ideal as it provided proximity to both St. James and Green Parks for his daily run, but was also large enough to make him less noticeable. Making certain that the front desk identified him as a businessman, he had made it a point to let them know that he was connected with Wal-Mart. The size and scope of the company was enough to give him legitimacy and a certain obscurity were anyone to casually run a check of company employees. Not only that, but on the way to the hotel he had fished out another passport in the name of William Reynolds, an actual employee of the company. As an executive, albeit a minor one, taking a suite would not seem out of the ordinary.

He unpacked his clothes and hung them neatly in the closet or folded in the drawers that he found behind a mirrored door. Looking around his suite, he suddenly felt lonely. Pulling out his cell he called Lila and told her he was out of the country for a few weeks and would see her when he returned. After he ended the call, he cursed himself for using an old phone that could be traced. Hopefully, one call would not be a disaster, but to prevent using it again, he removed the chip and smashed it. Satisfied that his tracks were covered well enough to provide a period of safety, Quint climbed into bed, pulled up the duvet and fell into dreamless sleep.

Chapter 3

Gerald Williams tapped his pen on his desk as he stared at the family portrait of his wife Jill and their two sons, James and George, both toddlers. He did not really see them. His thoughts kept churning around the question of who would put out a hit on Quinton Cord. To the best of his knowledge, neither he nor his superiors had told anyone of the latest assignment given to the code breaker. That meant someone leaked the information to either a government or individual that did not intend for Quint to succeed. Gerald was frustrated. Quint had disappeared without letting him know where and whether he would continue his assignment. As the handler, known to Quint as 'G', it was Gerald's responsibility to provide information, liaison, and protection for him. He answered only to the head of CIA and through him, the head of the committee for Homeland Security. Therefore the number of people who knew of the assignment was limited. With no choice, he picked up his phone and dialed the director. While Marshall Thomas was a curmudgeon of the first order, he was damned good at surviving Washington politics and had been for the last twenty years.

"Mr. Thomas, Gerald Williams here. Our man Cord has taken off for parts unknown. Seems someone doesn't like the idea of his latest assignment and tried to take him out. He got away unharmed and wasted no time going to ground."

"What the fuck! Have you talked to him?"

"Had an email transmission. Nothing more."

"Right. Get someone on it and see where the hell he popped off to." Thomas paused, "Any ideas on the hit man or who hired him?"

"That's the hell of it. I can't figure out who knew what he was working on that would have leaked it."

"Whatever it takes, I want Quinton Cord found and back on this. Try to re-establish contact while we are checking where he might have gone, and I'll have someone start looking for the leak. It's critical. Some of the info we are getting points to something big being planned by either ISIS or some unknown hostile and we don't know what or when. Breaking that damned code needs to happen fast."

"Yes sir, will do."

When Gerald hung up the phone, he immediately emailed Quint to let him know they were looking into the leak and who might be out to get him. He reiterated the importance of the assignment and the request for his whereabouts.

He finished typing a memo documenting the call and was ready to go to lunch, when the computer pinged letting him know he had an email.

"No can do!" was the total reply. Gerald stared at it before cursing. He couldn't blame the man, but quitting was something no one did with the Agency. While they might fire you, you did not quit on them, and you did not run out.

*****

Quint was cursing as well. Sitting at his computer he ran every code breaking tool he could think of and all came up blank. Pulling the coded message on top of the key paid he studied it for at least the fiftieth time. The fact that the numbers did not repeat made it more difficult. The only clues were the repeated dots and asterisks.

*57.*41.,210,319,11..*312,27,22,93,71,22.31,111,141,211,108,64,710.
69,910,15.178,1412,122,187,113,43,1612,127..*517,163,38,61,199,22
9,248,1014.*1728,48,63,192,167..*73,165,104,2419.153,193,1510,151
1,196,827..

Quint sat in thought before jotting down probabilities based on past experience. If he could intercept another message, he would be able to cross reference for repeated numbers or patterns and begin to make some sense of the code. He suspected it was based on some text that all parties had access to. Since it involved multiple nationalities, the odds were it was in English rather than Arabic or some other language. Tossing his pen down, he stood and stretched. Carefully locking his computer and documents in his small attaché, he tucked them into the room safe along with his passports and other items he did not want anyone to find.

He wished he could trust someone, but experience had taught him the lone wolf sometimes survived better alone than in a pack...and he was a lone wolf. Tugging on his ubiquitous London Fog to protect against a light mist, he checked his room to assure that anything that might be of use to identify his real mission was locked away, he hung the *Do Not Disturb* sign on the door, set his special trap that would let him know if someone entered while he was out, and walked to the elevator. He bypassed the desk, making sure the concierge was looking the other way, and quickly hurried out the door. From the hotel he walked to the St. James Park underground station and bought a return ticket for Paddington Station. He carried a newspaper under his arm that he pulled out when he reached his seat. He buried his nose in it to discourage conversation and to render himself more anonymous. At Paddington, he stuck the folded paper back under his arm and joined the throngs of people disembarking. It was a short walk to the bank of lockers in the station. Walking to the one he had rented for years, he entered his code and extracted a plain black satchel. Reversing his route, he returned to his hotel. After he checked the trip wire to assure that all was as he had left it, Quint entered his room and walked over to the desk where he opened the satchel.

He lifted out two flannel wrapped packages. In one was a SIG-Sauer P226 pistol and in the other an integrally silenced MP-10. In the bottom of the satchel were several stacks of extra magazines. He felt better with more firepower than that of the one weapon he brought with him from the States. Digging further in the satchel he found the matte-black knife with spring loaded five-inch blade. Beside that was a package of plastique and the needed ingredients for several bombs and two more cell phones that he needed to charge and have ready. Whoever the asshole was that had been put on his ass, Quint did not intend for him to nail him. If he got the chance, he was planning to take the shooter out and he would not wait for orders from Langley to do it. There were too many politicians and pencil pushers worried for their careers to ever appreciate the daily peril he put himself in when he signed a contract with the CIA. He had had an early awakening and he used it to develop as many ways as possible to assure self-protection. The CIA knew none of that. To them he was just a pansy-assed nerd that was as naive as a babe. He liked it that way. Now that he was essentially rogue, he didn't know what or from whom to expect the next threat. But he trusted his gut...it was coming.

Removing his laptop from the safe he then stowed the

weapons inside. He logged onto the Internet to connect with his handler. *"Hey "G," weather is fine in the Caribbean. I like it enough here I am retiring. Met a gorgeous chick. No more hunt and hunted games for me. I don't like the odds. It's been great. Wishing you all the best. Will send a Christmas card."*

Instantly his computer pinged, *"Fuck that. It doesn't work that way and you know it. You know too much and your skills are too needed for Langley to just kiss your sweet ass bye-bye. Where the hell are you and don't tell me it's the Caribbean. I'm not that gullible. You know I have always played straight with you. I can help you if you will let me. Don't piss the big boys off or it won't just be tangos coming after you."*

Quint sat in deep thought before replying: *"This is not about you. Someone somewhere is a mole. Until I know who that is and how this leak came about we are both better off if you don't know where I am. Not to worry, if I figure anything out I'll tell you. If you get any read on who's after me, I would rest easier knowing."*

"Maybe I could help now if I knew where you are. If you get in trouble, let me know. I don't won't to lose you, man. Just hang in there."

"I'll keep it in mind. In the meantime, I'm off to the beach."

From the moment he logged on until he logged off, the computer geeks at CIA worked to trace his signal. He would have been pleased to know that they were unable with SQL protocol to follow the network path that Lila created. Using satellite-tracing capabilities they would soon start tracking all cell phone transmissions and mapping any that went to "G." From that they would verify and establish the location of each one. Any contact they could not identify would be under immediate suspicion and investigated. He would not be using the Agency issued cell phone to call anyone stateside until he knew more about who was out to get him.

Quint picked up the code that lay beside the computer and again let it run through his mind. The asterisks could mean capitals if the dots really stood for periods, or they could refer to another text that was alternated between asterisks. The single dots could indicate the end of words. That seemed the most likely scenario. Did the double dots indicate the end of a sentence, or something else? He jotted down all of his questions and the possible answers to the ones he had analyzed. That done he logged onto the dark site used by the London cell to see if he could pick up any new transmissions. Leaving his computer running, he phoned room service to order lunch.

When the waiter arrived with a tray on a rolling cart, he tipped him and waited for the man to leave. Rolling the cart over to the desk, he positioned it so he could watch the computer while he ate his Plowman's Sandwich with chutney. The dark ale was perfect with it. He fell in love with the combo years before in a Salisbury pub when he visited there on vacation with his parents.

As he chewed he watched the chatter on the site. Nothing indicated more than routine propaganda to keep the minions enthralled by the vicious rhetoric of the militant zealots that had claimed the soul of Islam. He had been amazed to watch the unfettered rise of a small under-rated faction to one that held the western world in unease waiting for their next murderous attack on innocents. The televised beheadings, the rise of Sharia law in many European cities, and the latest attacks in Paris and Brussels had the governments of the free world reeling. Political correctness and do-gooders had all but brought democracy to its knees and given ISIS the space to flourish. Quint had grown cynical watching fumbling politicians who cared more about augmenting their images, egos, wallets, and careers than proactively protecting the country.

*****

At Langley, Gerald was musing about what to do with his code breaker. He could not blame him for doing a runner. If he were in the man's shoes, he would do the same thing. By the same token, he could not allow him to quit work on the damned code. It was simply too imperative that they break it. Searching his Rolodex, he flipped up the name he was looking for. There were other code breakers they had used in the past and while not as good, it at least gave them a back-up brain trying to solve the puzzle. He buzzed Marlowe and asked her to get Jeffrey Knotts on the line. He drummed his pencil while he waited. In less than a minute, she let him know to pick up the phone.

"Jeffrey." There was no need to identify himself as he had worked with the man in the field for years. "We need you to take a look at something we intercepted. It's a terrorist message and we need to get it cracked ASAP. Can you do it for us?"

"Sure. Same fee as always plus a bonus if I crack it." Jeffrey loved the challenges the codes provided almost as much as Quint. A former CIA agent, he had been forced to retire from the field when he was paralyzed from the waist down by a sniper's bullet. He hated terrorists with a passion for stealing his career from him. He had loved the thrill of fieldwork. It gave him an adrenalin rush like no other. During his long recovery, he utilized his time in bed to become an expert in computers and to research codes...a topic that had always fascinated him. When he discovered that he had a knack for it, he wasted no time letting the Agency know there was still something he could contribute. With a burning need for revenge he was glad to be back in the fray. "Send it on and I'll get right on it. And thanks. I was going nuts sitting here with nothing to do but eat, piss, and shit."

"No problem. Thanks, man. I know it has been tough for you since that mission went south. You were the best we had out there." The pencil Gerald was playing with snapped. He dropped the pieces in the trash.

"Hey, I was just staying alive. The second string doesn't last long in this business. I still would like to find the son of a bitch that leaked the details to ISIS. I'm just lucky they didn't kill me like they thought, although at the time I sure as hell didn't feel lucky." Jeffrey paused, "Did you ever get a lead on the mole that outed me?"

"Still working on it. You know I would tell you if we had."

Marlowe buzzed him the minute they hung up to let him know the director was on the line. Gerald groaned before picking it up. The man had a way of irritating the hell out of him.

"Yes, sir."

"We think we have a lead. Perkins did a comb of Cord's file and after some additional digging pulled up something that might tell us where Cord scurried off to. Seems he inherited a place on Figure Eight Island on the coast of North Carolina when his parent died. The records show he sold it. An attorney for a blind corporation Cord's father created had handled the sale for Cord. The new deed is in the name of a Jefferson Quarls. Jefferson was Cord's mother's maiden name. Maybe a dead end, but it's all we have right now. It seems our Mr. Cord got wary after that first attempt to take him out, so who knows what else the wily bastard did to throw up smokescreens." Marshall Thomas growled, "At least Perkins is doing something to come up with some answers."

Gerald could read the veiled criticism in that comment. He bit his lip to keep from telling the pompous ass to fuck off. He felt no need to tell Thomas he had done something besides twiddle his thumbs. And he was past letting the bastard know how much he needled him. There relationship had been cold since Marshall threw him under the bus to take the heat off himself and the Agency when a congressional investigation into CIA interrogation tactics was raising a stink in D.C. Marshall Thomas had set it up at the President's directive, however the upper echelon was not about to acknowledge complicity. Gerald was just far enough down the ladder without being too far to fit the bill. He became the red meat for the "Congressional Pit Bulls"...a group of Senators and Representatives that despised the CIA because they couldn't control it. After the Department of Justice succeeded in stonewalling and delaying, something else popped up to take the heat off him and the whole thing fizzled out to nothing. At the time, he had realized the necessity for taking the fall, but he felt that Marshall was still angry with him for the interrogation of the Saudi terror suspect that ended in the man's death. The fact that the man had plans for dirty bombing the White House and Capitol was not enough to warrant the accidental death in the eyes of many. A bigger man than Thomas, the President had called to thank him personally for foiling the bombing plot and taking the rap before the Congressional committee. He looked down at the two halves of the pencil he had been tapping. It was snapped in half. Gerald forced his voice to dispassion, "Was there anything else, sir?"

"Well, hell! Do you think I called you just to chat? Get on it and see if Figure Eight is where Cord is holed up."

"I'll have one of our Wilmington agents check it out."

"No. You're going. We're not dicking around with this."

"I thought you didn't want him to know my identity."

"Fuck it. It doesn't matter what you call yourself or if he knows who you are. I just told your secretary to book you on a flight tonight, so best go home and grab your things. You don't have a lot of time."

"I'm on my way." Gerald hung up seething. It was just like the asshole to undermine him with his own secretary.

Gerald called his wife to have her pack his bag and have it waiting for him. He then gathered his things and stuffed a few files in his briefcase to study on the plane. Satisfied he had everything he needed, he stopped at his secretary's desk to let her know he was leaving. Marlowe gave him the flight details and the boarding passes she had printed out for him. She waited until he was gone before entering his office and opening his computer. Knowing his password, she wasted no time logging on and reading his emails. She had already monitored his calls.

Marlowe Hollins was a beautiful woman and an efficient secretary. She loved her job and her new husband and would do anything in her power to keep them. Marlowe had the life she had always dreamed of and thought would never be hers. As a prostitute and homeless teen hooked on cocaine, her world had turned on finding the next high and doing whatever it took to afford it. At twenty a local pastor took her under his wing, financed her at the local community college and supported her until she could break away from her old life. She owed her very existence to Rev. Robin Downey and his wife Carole. With the secretarial skills from college courses and a one-way bus ticket to Washington, she left Little Rock far behind. An Internet search turned up a name she would use instead of the one she had been born with, Mary Higgins. Her new identity was good enough to get her a job at the Agency, especially with Gerald's wife to vouch for her when she ran into her at a coffee shop. Striking up a conversation, the two women were soon friends. When his wife told Gerald about the woman she had met and really liked, he took her suggestion and hired Marlowe immediately to replace his secretary of many years who was retiring. He had thought about doing a more thorough check on her than he had, but everything seemed on the up and up in her application and the initial security check.

Unfortunately for Marlowe and Gerald, her past was not quite behind her.

She had started working for the Agency shortly after her arrival. Several weeks after being hired by the Agency she met her future husband at a bar near his doctor's office. They hit it off immediately and within months married. She did not think her life could have been more perfect...and then, the past rose up and bit her in the ass. A former client recognized her and threatened to tell her husband about her checkered past unless she agreed to be a pipeline of information for him. She hated sneaking. She hated betraying her boss. He was a decent man and did not deserve her spying. She hated betraying her friendship with Jill, his wife. She hated not knowing what kind of harm she was doing giving her blackmailer what he demanded. She just knew it could not be good, despite the man's claims that it was nothing more than a need to know due to his position. If that were the case she pondered, why wasn't he in the chain of information already?

She had just logged off and risen from the desk when she heard footsteps approaching the closed door. "Shit," she swore under her breath.

"Mrs. Hollins, did you need something?" Gerald asked when he found her in his office.

"I misplaced a file and thought I might find it on your desk. It wasn't important, but I still don't like not being able to find it."

"Not here then?"

"No, unfortunately," she shrugged.

"Well, no doubt it will turn up." Gerald walked over to his desk and removed something that was hidden from her by his body. He slipped it into his pocket before turning to leave. "Forgot something and thought it wouldn't be a bad idea to have it."

"Enjoy your trip." She smiled as she followed him out of his office and back to her desk. Marlowe was shaken. Please, God, she prayed, don't let him suspect me.

Gerald was far too preoccupied to worry about his secretary, and did not especially note that she had been in his office. He saw nothing suspicious in that and he trusted her. At the moment he focused his total concern on Quint's safety and potentially his own. He had returned to his office for the 9 MM Beretta pistol he rarely carried since leaving fieldwork. As a desk jockey he had always assumed he was in a safe, low profile job. Now he wasn't so sure. With his special clearance, taking a gun on the flight was not a problem. He just hoped he didn't need it. He had worked in the field long enough to take care of himself in most situations. It would help if he knew what he was up against though. He didn't like going into the unknown.

Chapter 4

Nemesis had been cooling his heels for days and he was nervous. His handler had told him to sit tight until further notice. He didn't know if he was just a sitting duck waiting to be taken out because of his failed attempt to kill the code breaker, or if there were more information pending that would allow him to finalize the job. He hoped it was the latter.

Nemesis was pacing his room at the Crabtree Marriott in Raleigh when he received the awaited call. It took him less than fifteen minutes to check out and start the two-hour drive to Wilmington and Figure Eight Island. He hoped the hit he was after would be there so he could wrap up this job and go onto the next one. He was relieved the man that hired him was still willing to give him work despite the failure in Raleigh. Nemesis didn't worry about the whys and what ifs, he just needed to do the wet work on Figure Eight, get paid, and move on to the next kill in Alexandria. He could not afford any more misses. Once he had accomplished the hits and collected his money, he planned to lay low for a long time. His line of work carried one overriding hazard: he could just as easily become the target to keep him quiet.

Using the Google Earth application on his phone, he pulled up the address on Figure Eight. He noted that access to the island required going through a security gate and that he had no intention of doing. He figured he would find a boat on the mainland side, steal it, and approach from the beach a short way down and out of sight of the target's house. Using the application, he scanned the shore of the mainland looking for a boat dock or boathouse. He spotted a likely one and zoomed in on it. With luck the owners of the property were not full time residents, so he could take the boat without anyone being the wiser.

It was dark when he reach the property he had identified using Google. Driving past he scanned the house and was relieved to see it was dark. Judging by the yellowing, rain-soaked flyers scattered in the drive, it appeared that no one had been in residence for some time. Pulling in to the drive he drove to the rear of the property and parked the car so it was out of sight of the street. Bushes along both sides of the lot screened the back area from any neighboring houses. Nemesis sat in the car for five minutes to make sure no one was aware of his presence and interested in coming to look. When all remained quiet, he grabbed his satchel containing the weapons he would need, locked his car and scurried down to the boat that was moored to a small pier.

Soon the tarp was peeled back and stowed out of the way. Then he began a methodical search of the boat. In the front stowage inside a bail bucket he found the ignition key. He chuckled to himself at just how easy it all was. So far everything was going smoothly. Untying the mooring line from the cleat, he pushed away from the dock. He allowed the current to carry the boat out into the water of the inland waterway before he dared to start the motor. Gunning the engine, he arced toward the property on the opposite shore where he anticipated finding his mark.

As he drew nearer the large cottage, he cut the engine and allowed the current to carry the boat toward the shore. When he was still a few yards out, he jumped over the side and towed the boat to shore where he hid it in marsh grass to the right of the large garden that surrounded the house. Palms and shrubbery along the property line would give him good cover as he staked out the cottage and planned his shot. Only the guesthouse showed any lights, so it was there that he expected to find his man. A dog's sharp barking was quickly silenced by someone in the house. Nemesis hated dogs.

Again the dog erupted into a frenzy of barking and again he was hushed. Nemesis squatted in the bushes underneath a large window and peered under the blind that covered all but an inch at the bottom. He could make out the legs of a man and another set that belonged to a woman. He could not see the dog but the dog was very aware of him judging by the low, menacing growl that the man's sharp command did not stop.

"I'm going to put him on his leash out back. That rabbit he's been chasing must be nosing around out there."

A woman's exasperated voice, interrupted, "For goodness sake, we will never get any peace if he barks at the damned rabbit all night. Why not put him in the garage along with some food? The rabbit will move on and then maybe he will shut up."

"Already, all right. Just don't get your dander up. I know you don't like him in the house and the dog knows it, too."

Nemesis settled against the foundation of the house and waited while the man took the dog into the adjoining garage. When the man returned, he was ready. With the silencer attached to his Glock semi-automatic, Nemesis strafed the room. The window shattered around him scattering glass all over the ground. He continued firing until nothing moved.

Using the barrel of his gun, he peered through the window at the bodies of an elderly couple. "Shit. The fucking caretakers!" Since the breaking window made enough noise to arouse anyone in the main house and all had remained quiet, he assumed that no one else was on the property. The dog was howling like he was demon possessed. Stowing his gun in the satchel, he dashed for the boat. Behind him he heard the sound of breaking glass and then the furious barking of the dog. Somehow the animal had broken out. Adding urgency to his escape, Nemesis had just made it into his boat and pushed from shore when the dog leaped into the water and began to swim after him. He fired but missed.

Gunning the engine, he raced across the water to the dock on the opposite bank. When he got to the dock, he tied the boat up, hefted the satchel and ran for his car. His tires spun gravel as he backed up and wheeled around to race out into the street. With his lights out, he was almost hit by a car approaching from the left. The other driver honked his horn in irritation as he swerved out of the way. When he reached 17, Nemesis turned on his lights and raced towards Interstate 140. If he rushed he would be in Alexandria before daylight. He did not intend to report another failure until he had one good hit. Figure Eight was bad intelligence apparently so he didn't feel he was to blame, but his handler was losing patience. He could not afford to miss in Alexandria.

*****

Still cursing from almost being sideswiped, Gerald stopped at the security gate onto the island and showed his CIA badge. The guard was not one to argue with that kind of ID. Following the guard's directions, he drove to the address he wanted and pulled into the driveway of an elegant house. The ocean made a dark backdrop for the estate. Light streamed from the window of what he assumed to be a guesthouse. Using it as a beacon, he had just stuck his leg out of the open door of his car when a large German Shepherd lunged forward barking furiously. Beating a hasty retreat, Gerald sat in his car wondering what to do next. Sorting through his glove box, he found his bottle of powerful pepper spray. He hated to use the stuff as it was seriously nasty, but he didn't see any other option since no one had appeared from the house to call the dog off.

Easing the window down, he sprayed the dog. A whining animal replaced the snarling beast in less than a heartbeat. He watched the dog race to the ocean. With the dog momentarily out of the way, Gerald trotted towards the back of the guesthouse where the light appeared to originate. Rounding the corner, he gaped in amazement at the broken window. Glass covered the ground like glistening shards of ice. He hurried over to investigate. Peering through the slats of the broken blinds, he spotted two bodies surrounded by pools of blood. Gerald brushed the glass from the windowsill and climbed into the room. He was careful to disturb nothing. The multiple gunshots sustained by both bodies indicated they had died almost instantly. Gerald skirted the bodies and gave a quick inspection to the rest of the small cottage. From there he entered the adjoining garage and saw another broken window. Judging by the water bowl and bag of dog food in the corner, the dog had broken out of here when the shots went off in the cottage.

Opening the far door, he entered the main house. He used his small but powerful flash light to walk from room to room of the tastefully decorated mansion. It did not appear that anyone had used it for a while. Ending his search in the kitchen, he glanced around again. He spotted a wastebasket near the door and on the off chance it had not been emptied, he walked over and started churning through the trash. A piece of paper caught his attention. Picking it up he turned it over, brushed off the crumbs and began to read: *"Thank you for taking such good care of me Mattie. I know Code is an imposition, but I hated to leave him in a kennel. I'll make it up to you when I return. Love to you and Percy...Q."*

Gerald shook his head. It was a sad business to be in. He loved it on most days, considered it vital to the nation's security, but there were times when it was a total bitch. This was one of them. He was furious that this innocent old couple had been so callously murdered. He was angry that as a desk jockey he had to turn over the hunt for the killer to someone else when in the past he would have been in the thick of the fray. He was sad that it would be up to him to let Quint know what happened. Judging by the note, these were people he loved. And then there was the dog to consider. He could not just leave the animal to starve, and he damned sure didn't know how to go about capturing him and getting him back to Washington.

Keeping the spray handy, Gerald traced his way back through the house. He paused just long enough to pick up two dog toys before climbing out the window in the room with the bodies. He would call the Agency to come in and mop up the scene, but he doubted they would find anything to identify the killer. Judging by the caliber of the spent shells, this was a professional job. He eased around the corner of the house searching for Quint's dog. After the hosing down he had given the poor animal, he doubted Code was going to want anything to do with him.

He found Code curled up by the back door of the main house. The dog whimpered when he walked up and began to cringe away from him. Gerald made his voice soft and reassuring as he slowly stretched out his hand with the toys and allowed them to drop with a soft plop. "Poor Code. I was mean to you, but you about scared the shit out of me boy. Come on and let me take you with me until we can find Quint."

At the mention of his name and that of his owner, Code's ears perked up. "That's right, Code, I'm going to take good care of you until we can get you back to Quint."

Code gave him a suspicious look when Gerald reached down to retrieve the toys he had clamped his jaws around.

He had no intention of fighting the dog for them, "That's fine. You can keep them. Come on, Code. Let's go."

He whistled and backed up waiting to see if the dog would rise and follow him. Code just stared and waited. Again he snapped his fingers and whistled, "Let's go find Quint, boy."

Code cocked his head to one side and studied him for long minutes. Sweat was beginning to break out on Gerald's brow when the dog slowly stood up and walked over to him. He put his toys down at Gerald's feet. Picking them up, Gerald stuck them in his pocket as the dog followed him back to the rental car. So much for the return flight. With a dog to deal with, he would have to drive. In Rocky Mount, Gerald left Interstate 95 and pulled into a service station where he bought a packaged sandwich and a Coke for himself and some water for Code. When he returned to the car, the dog watched him open his sandwich and then began growling.

"Okay, okay, I get the message." Carefully rewrapping his sandwich, he walked back into the station and selected a ham and cheese for the dog. When he returned to the car Code was licking the last of Gerald's tuna salad sandwich from his lips. Gerald hated ham and cheese and now he was stuck with eating it. "Dammit, Code, we're going to have to establish some ground rules. Number one is: I don't eat your food and you don't eat mine."

Gerald could have sworn the dog grinned at him as he unwrapped the sandwich and struggled to eat it. After the first half, he gave up and handed the remainder to Code who gobbled it down in two big gulps. Gerald drove back onto I-95, wondering how he was going to explain the new houseguest to his wife. His kids were another matter. They would love the dog and not want to give him up. With a full stomach and obvious trust in his new caretaker, Code curled up in the backseat and was soon snoring. Gerald swore. He now not only had a dog to tend to, but the animal snored like an old freight train chugging out of the station. He hoped to hell Quint would relieve him of the dog in short order.

Frustrated by the talk radio show on the radio, he snapped it off. That was the trouble with the country as far as he was concerned. There were too many oblivious, head in the sand, do-gooders with no appreciation for the danger the country faced; and too many egotistical, power hungry politicians ready to use them to climb the ladder in Washington. Marshall Thomas was one of them. He was shrewd and capable, but he had an ambitious streak a mile wide and an unhealthy fear of crossing politicians. Gerald knew beyond a doubt that Thomas would not hesitate to throw his ass under the bus again, or anyone else's if it saved his own ass or helped his climb in the Washington hierarchy.

He toyed with the idea of starting a private company that contracted with governmental agencies for the kind of work they wanted to distance themselves from to keep their own noses clean. He had used some of these companies before for work that needed to be under the radar. With friends in them, mostly retired CIA, FBI, SEALs, and some Green Berets and other special forces, he could join one of those firms. His hesitation once his kids came along was for their safety, and that of his own hide as a father and husband. He wasn't a coward so much as a realist. People who played around in that arena were courting a short lifespan. But then, he wondered, was he any less of a target. The bad guys knew him by reputation as a real bad ass and the politicians didn't give a fuck if his job put him or his family in danger. That piss-ant salary they paid him was half what he could make in the private arena and he would not be tied to a desk when he wanted to be in the thick of things. The more he thought about his toady of a boss, that little dick of a man, the angrier he became. Marshall Thomas resented that Gerald had the respect of the men in the field...others like Gerald who had put their lives on the line for the country they had sworn to defend. These, the finest fighting men in the country's arsenal, did not give a rat's ass for Washington politics and game players. For them, it was about doing whatever it took to keep the homeland safe. If that meant playing dirty, so be it.

When he walked into his house, Jill was asleep on the sofa in the den. The minute she heard his footsteps she sat up and hugged him.   "What are you doing with that animal in my house?"

"It's a long story, Baby Cakes. Can it keep until morning? I'm too bushed to get into it now."

"Put that dog in the garage and let's go to bed." Jill smiled at her husband, "I'm just glad to have you home. But, that dog is another issue."

Gerald reached down and tugged her hand to help her rise, "Somehow, I knew it would be."

Jill studied him before softly remarking, "You've had a tough day. I can see it in your face."

"Worse than. I wish I could tell you about it, but believe me, you don't want to know."

"Goes with the turf, but I love you any way. Now let's go to bed and we'll see if I can find a way to cheer you up."

Gerald laughed, "No question about that."

Chapter 5

Quint had just walked out of the shower following a five-mile run around Green Park when the computer pinged letting him know he had email. Draping the towel around his neck, he walked over and signed on. The message was terse: *"Quint, you must call me. It's about Figure Eight. You don't want me to do this one by email. I have your dog. And enough of the "G' business. My name is Gerald."*

Quint shivered and it wasn't from the water drying on his nude body. Something was bad wrong if his handler had Code. *"Thanks, Gerald. Leave the office and get a throw away phone, then email me the number. I'll call you."*

"I'll pick one up on the way to work. Give me an hour or so."

"Okay, later. And go to a park or somewhere your call can't be picked up by a remote microphone." When Quint logged off, he badly wanted to phone the Hendersons and see why Code was no longer with them, but deep down he sensed there would be no answer even if he dared to call. He wondered who had figured out the cottage was his and why they would have killed two innocent people. Whoever wanted him dead was serious. Too on edge to sit, he paced the floor as he waited for Gerald to contact him with the cell number.

Gerald bought the phone and drove down George Washington Memorial Parkway. Instead of turning right to go to his office in the main building, he made a left turn and took Turkey Loop Road to the north end where it petered out. Parking his car in the edge of the woods, he picked his way down the bluff and across the Potomac Heritage Trail to the river. He gazed across the rapids to the opposite shore and the marshy banks of Chatauqua Island. It looked so peaceful in the early morning sun. He was composing his thoughts on how to break the sad news of the deaths at Quint's beach house, when his personal cell phone rang. He glanced down at it, recognizing the number. He answered it, happy to delay the talk with Quint as long as he could.

"Jeffrey, what's up man?"

"Some son of a bitch just tried to off me."

"Holy shit! Are you hurt?"

"My pride maybe, other than that I'm just pissed."

"What happened?" Hearing this from Jeffrey, Gerald was glad Quint had ducked out. There were some serious leaks and people determined to protect the coded messages, people that had no compunction about killing.

"If I didn't trust my gut, I'd be dead. Something raised the hackles on my neck. So I rolled onto the floor just as a spray of bullets slammed through the window. I grabbed my gun and crawled over and fired off several rounds in the direction of the shooter. I think I hit the bastard. I found blood outside but no body. I must not have wounded him too badly as he got away. If my damned legs still worked, I would have chased the fucker and killed him."

Gerald shook his head. A man in a wheelchair had some serious guts to want to go after a killer. "You need to come in. I'm sending a car. Buster will pick you up and get you out of there, ASAP. Grab what you need to lay low for a while."

"Will do. And see if you can get someone to fix my window and secure things here for me."

Gerald called Buster Walton, a former SEAL and private operative he contracted for under-the-radar operations. He explained what he needed and was assured that Jeffrey Knotts would be at Langley in twenty minutes. Buster and Jeffrey had been with him on numerous operations, including the one when Jeffrey was injured. They all remained friends and met occasionally to have a cold one. They had been a formidable team, what one lacked another made up for. Between them they were fluent in ten languages and could get by in five more. When Buster needed someone to hack a computer, Jeffrey was his go-to guy. He was as pissed as Gerald when he learned someone tried to kill Jeffrey.

If anyone could get Jeffrey out it would be Buster. He was like a one-man army, strong as an ox, quick, and intuitive. He could analyze a situation in seconds and react with deadly force. He was also a first-rate sniper. There was no finesse about Buster when he was riled, which explained why he left the SEALs. One damn stupid order too many for the sole purpose of maintaining political cover had resulted in him blowing his top to his commander just after he handed in his resignation. His commander, Roger Brice, had agreed with him and wished him luck. Although Brice had been following orders, he hated some of them with a passion. Most of the guys in the field, including Brice, had a serious contempt for meddling politicians who gave orders with no knowledge of the realities of what these men were doing to keep the country safe. Sometimes they thought the politicos were more the enemy than anyone else.

Gerald looked down at the throwaway phone and took a deep breath. He needed to get the call to Quint over with and get into the office. He typed the phone number into his cell phone email system and sent it to Quint. His new phone rang seconds later.

Quint wasted no time asking, "What's going on? Why is Code with you?"

"My boss got a read on your ten-twenty, or so he thought. They tracked the transfer of your beach house into a bogus name. Figuring it was you, they sent me down there to bring you into protective custody. I'm sorry to have to tell you this, but some asshole murdered your caretakers before I could get there."

"Oh, my God, I knew it. They did not deserve to die. I hate myself for bringing anyone else into this mess. I'm going to have to come back and arrange a funeral. They have no one else. I'm the closest thing to family they had."

"I've already made arrangements for the bodies. When this cools down you can do a memorial service. Right now *I don't even want to know where you are*; and it damned sure would not be smart to show up. Just be careful. There are surveillance cameras on just about every corner worldwide. They are in the airports, too. It won't be long until your face pops up on one of them. Until we know who is after you and who is leaking, you need to stay under the radar."

"Yeah, I know. I'm doing my best. Now what about my dog?"

"Code and my boys are new best friends. As for my wife, it's going to take a nice piece of jewelry to buy myself back in her favor and I'm sending you the bill." Gerald chuckled.

"No problem. I just appreciate knowing Code wasn't left behind."

"One more thing you need to know. Another code breaker I use was attacked early this morning. He's damn lucky to be alive."

"Shit. Someone's stirred up a hornet's nest. As for me I have three goals right now: staying alive, cracking the damned code, and as soon as that's done, I'm going to kill the son of a bitch that wasted the Hendersons. Any lead on the shooter?" Quint's voice was tight with anger and suppressed grief.

"Not yet. I'll keep you posted. When we hang up, I'm ditching this phone in the river. I bought three more under different names. If I need to contact you by phone I will email you the number from a throw away. I suggest you dump the phone you are using as well, and get another."

"Already thought of that." Quint paused, "Thanks for seeing to the Hendersons for me. Put the biggest wreath of flowers you can find on their graves and I'll pay you back as soon as I can."

"I'm sorry as I can be about this, so you don't need to pay me for the flowers. I damn well intend for Langley to cover all expenses." Gerald cleared his throat, "Where would you like them buried?"

Quint gave him the name and numbers of the family plot in Oakwood Cemetery in Raleigh. It was just a short way down on the right from that of Elizabeth Edwards, wife of former vice-presidential candidate John Edwards. "I want them with my parents. For the last few years they've been like family to me. Even before my parents' deaths, there were times when I was closer to them than my own parents. I'll miss them...badly"

Quint paused. Gerald could tell he was trying to choke back tears. He waited for him to continue. "I wonder if you could find someone reliable to look after the place for me until I can get back?"

"Our North Carolina office is already on it. They will keep it secured and monitored just in case the son-of-a-bitch figures out he got the wrong ones and decides to come back."

"After chalking up three strikes, I suspect he will disappear and a new killer will be after my ass and your other guy, too."

"That's a possibility, Quint."

After saying goodbye, Gerald stood and heaved the phone into the river. It crashed on rocks and the shattered pieces were quickly swirled away. He climbed the bluff and returned to his car. He didn't know it, but miles up the river a body rested in the bushes along the shore where crabs and birds were already working on it. With the face blown off and the feeding frenzy of local wildlife, no one was going to do a fast ID, and unless it was found soon the tide would carry it towards the bay.

*****

The man who had ordered the hit on Quint and Jeffrey was pissed. The last shooter had been an incompetent idiot. This problem must be resolved before the CIA succeeded in cracking the code. That he could not afford. Everything would be ruined if his years of careful planning fell through. He picked up the phone and talked in a muffled voice. No one must know his plan. The new shooter would either succeed or he too would be replaced. Idiots all. None were as powerful or as intelligent as he. He chuckled to himself. None had his cunning. He had assumed a name and identity, moved to a new location, and steadily worked up the ranks of local politics. He was now in Washington, the center of U.S. power. Though he did not yet hold the reins, he intended to. With the latest election he was just steps away from the presidency. It was not an insurmountable problem. He laughed at the stupidity of the American people...so gullible, so naive, so trusting. They were like lambs jumping off the cliff, too busy with their silly pursuits to really bother with who they elected as long as he was likeable. Godless infidels one and all...they deserved what was coming. It was Allah's plan. With his rise to power, the world would be on its way to unity under the one true religion. Now he just needed to get the snag in Paris worked out and he would pull the trigger on the operation. Alhumdulillah! *Praise be to God!*

That piece of ass he had enjoyed in Little Rock was proving to be even better as an informant than as a prostitute. She was so fucking scared she was feeding him everything. Sometimes he knew what was going on before her boss did. The latest intel from her was worrisome. Apparently her boss was beginning to use his home phone and computer more. He would have his guy figure out a way to tap into those.

*****

When Quint hung up the phone with Gerald, the first thing he did was cry like a heartbroken little boy. The Hendersons had always been there for him from the time he was a child. When his father hurt his feelings by calling him "Sissy Quincey," or demeaned him in some way, it was to them he ran. Mattie would hold him and murmur sweet and loving things in his ear to console; and when she had him calm, Percy would make him laugh. Their loss left a gaping hole in his life. There was now no one to give him selfless, pure love and comfort. When he had cried himself out, he stood. He would avenge their deaths. The shooter and the asshole that hired him were limited in time on this side of the dirt if he had his say.

But first, he had to crack the code. He was frustrated that everything that had come through so far was typical chatter. No matter how many times, he pored over that damned coded message he could not figure it out. He badly needed another message, or some other clue.

Pacing the room, he decided it was time to change identity and move to another hotel. The call that he had made to Lila nagged at him. It was possible that someone could have traced his location if they had were tracking that call. He called the desk and told them to prepare his bill and charge it to his card. He would make the conversion to his new identity, walk out the front door, and relocate. He needed to pick another hotel that would allow him the opportunity to enjoy the nearby parks. With that in mind, he went on the Internet and found the one he wanted. He reserved a room on line, before going to the bathroom to once again transform into some one else.

Leonard White of Charlotte, NC, checked into the Royal Garden Hotel in Kensington. He had selected it because of a suite that offered a view of Kensington Gardens and the adjacent Hyde Park. The Connaught and Grosvenor House were tempting, but he decided he did not need to be quite that close to the US Embassy. With a close shave, hair graying at the temples, and blue contact lenses, he looked nothing like the much heavier mustachioed man that walked out of the Millennium Hotel earlier that morning.

At the front desk he casually mentioned he owned an investment business and was in London to research real estate opportunities for his clients. After he tipped the porter that carried his bags to his room, Quint looked around the suite.

The Art Deco decor was not his preference, however it was tasteful, pleasant, clean, and comfortable. The best feature was the desk with WiFi that overlooked the Round Pond in Kensington Park. He admired the view for several minutes before beginning the task of unpacking and setting up his computer. He didn't have the heart to deal with anything more. He needed a good run to cleanse his soul of the evil that surrounded him and had hurt those he loved. He regretted that Code was not there to run with him.

The day was cool and overcast with rain-heavy clouds adding a humidity level that was uncomfortable despite the relatively low temperature. He returned to his room wet with perspiration. After a cool shower, he toweled off, put on his sweats and sat at the desk. Logging onto the web, he began searching the sites that he was monitoring. He decided all were just chatter, except for one. It was the phrase *'stay tuned for Tony the Tiger'* that jumped out at him. He emailed Gerald to run a check to see if prior to the first coded transmission whether or not the same phrase had preceded it. If he did not hear back by ten o'clock, he would email Lila to work on it for him. She would be through at the university by then due to the five-hour time difference.

An hour later, Quint still had not heard back and was growing restless. While he waited he picked up the phone and rang room service. He was starving after the run, but he didn't want to leave the room to go out for dinner for fear Gerald would email while he was out. Even more importantly, he was waiting to see if another coded message showed up. He was still waiting when his dinner arrived. Settling down to his Shepard's Pie, green salad, and a bottle of Pinot Noir, Quint relaxed for the first time that day. The dinner was superb and the wine perfect with it, as was the Tarte Tatin for dessert.

He felt the best he had all day. If Lila were nearby, he would call and arrange to see her. He thought of going down and picking up someone in the bar to relieve that particular itch, but the idea wasn't appealing...not nearly as appealing as Lila. He needed to watch that. He wondered if he was developing feelings for her that he could not afford to have. So far she had been tolerant if not happy about their arrangement, so it was up to him to squelch any desire for more.

Turning on the television, he watched the local BBC newscast for a half hour. An upcoming meeting of the Queen with members of Parliament received top billing. The date was already selected for a few days away. Quint began channel-surfing to find the local CNN to see what the lead story was there. It looked as though France was planning something at the Presidential Palace where various Heads of State would be invited to meet with the President of France, however the date was not yet finalized. In the US, President Clayton Northrup was speaking at a fund raiser for his Vice-President who was pursuing the presidency in the upcoming election. The speech was slated for a little later in the month. The weatherman came on announcing that the UK was in for a rainy spell. *Wonderful,* Quint thought, *what else is new?*

Using the remote, he clicked off the TV and stood looking out at Kensington Park. Rain was falling rendering the view gray and dismal. A few people were walking in the area closest to the street, all angling umbrellas towards the wind. Quint sat back down at the desk and stared at the computer screen. As though Gerald heard him willing a response, the computer pinged. The email he was awaiting arrived. Opening it, Quint read: *"Yes. Same sentence preceded coded message by a day. Looks like you may be onto something. Keep me posted. Nothing yet on who hired the killer; however a body was discovered yesterday in the Potomac that appears to be that of a known assassin. He may or may not be the one that tried to kill you and my other guy. Stay safe...Gerald."*

Chapter 6

Prince Fayed Abdullah studied the handsome United States Democratic Speaker of the House, Douglas Forsyth. He knew him for the ambitious, power-hungry man that had no brakes when he was after a goal...and now he was after the ultimate one. His veneer of polish and charm was just that, a convenient mask for screening the man beneath, a man with a facile tongue and a false identity, one designed to hide his Saudi birth. Fayed had no problem with that as long as the man shared his own ambitions. Both men were frustrated. He was just one in a long line of royal princes in the Saudi kingdom and his chances of rising to the top would have been minimal were it not for one thing. He was one of the wealthiest men in the world thanks to his father's business acumen. What wealth his father had not made in oil, playing currency and stock markets had. Fayed used the cadre of financial wizards accumulated by his late father, not only to maintain the vast financial empire but also to expand it. He was many times over a billionaire. One might not think as much judging by the relative modesty of his attire and home, however one stare into those unsettling dark eyes was enough to assure that he was a ruthless and powerful man that would stop at nothing to obtain what he wanted. What he wanted was the ability to manipulate U.S. policy to his advantage and to use that power to become the ruler of his country. With his cousin as President, he would control the U.S. as well.

Forsyth fidgeted in his chair. It was critical that he gain the financial backing he needed for the next phase of his political career. While the trip to Saudi Arabia was for the ostensible purpose of a trade agreement on oil prices, the underlying motive was far more important to him. Looking away from Fayed's intent stare, Forsyth studied the palms that lined the wall in front of the Prince's property. In the distance the sea sparkled in the glaring sunlight. It was a palatial estate compared to the compounds on either side, but not what one might expect of a royal Saudi with one of the largest fortunes in the world. There were no huge yachts moored in the manmade harbor in front, only a forty-five foot powerful cabin cruiser.

A dry breeze lifted Forsyth's sprayed hair and he unconsciously reached up and patted it in place. He was a meticulous man in politics, grooming, and his personal life. His wife was a perfect example of a politically suited spouse: beautiful but not flashy, socially poised, quiet, unassuming, and thoroughly cowed by his domineering.

Looking back at Fayed, Forsyth struggled to find the words he needed to convey the real purpose of his trip without divulging too much. The Prince already had far more knowledge about his former life than Forsyth would have liked. He dared not allow the Saudi to gain the advantage of even more leverage. As it was, they had a detente of a kind. Few knew that the Prince was a homosexual. Most of those that learned of his leanings were now experiencing eternal rest. Forsyth's ambition was greater than any fastidiousness about his sexuality, thus he and the Prince had been intimate on several occasions. As far as he was concerned it gave him a firm hold over the Prince. However, Forsyth was glad the Arab was enamored of his adolescent houseboy at the moment, and thus not interested in him sexually. In a land where sexual deviation was anathema, Fayed could not afford for his proclivities to be revealed. If the Prince were not so eager for him to obtain his goal, Forsyth doubted he would have survived those few trysts, cousin or not. That was especially true after watching the Prince casually strangle an unwilling sex slave when both men were high on a potent mixture of alcohol and cocaine. After that, Douglas never touched cocaine again despite continuing to drink. He figured he deserved some escape from pressure.

"Ah, Douglas, or perhaps I should use your former name Ali...I have rarely seen you at such a loss for words. If I may be so bold as to suggest the reason you requested this little reunion. Assuming, of course, it is not for amorous reasons." Fayed raised his left eyebrow and smirked. "Perhaps it is my deep pockets you need more than my prick?"

Forsyth felt a blush suffuse his face at the coarse comment. "I wouldn't use quite those words." He swallowed hard before he continued, "You know how much I enjoyed our times together. However, you are right. I need serious money in order to execute plans that are in place to achieve the goals we both desire...plans that require expensive talent."

"I see. And my reward for such generosity?" The Prince enjoyed toying with him, much like a cat with a tasty mouse struggling in his claws.

"When I am President, I will see to it that your country realizes you would make a better King than our cousin. I will also use all of the resources at my disposal to make Saudi Arabia the predominate nation in this region with greater territory than you have now."

"That is most tempting. And how much will this marvelous

future cost me?" Fayed leaned back in his chair and casually crossed his legs as he waited. He was prepared to pay a lot, but Forsyth did not need to know how much. He would buy him as cheaply as he could. And the strings he tied to the money would be very secure indeed.

"For starters, thirty-five million."

"These must be very talented gentlemen indeed. I'm not prepared to be that generous, unfortunately."

"Then part for now and more later. Less than twenty-five it will make it impossible to proceed. After the first steps are complete, it will take millions more to secure my position. Thirty-five million is a conservative estimate I assure you, especially with what it will cost to run for the Presidency."

Fayed leaned forward and tapped him on the knee, "You will have twenty-five deposited in a Swiss account before you leave. Now, lets finalize my requirements."

Douglas walked to the black limousine that waited on the tile paved courtyard behind the Prince's beach house. He felt the hackles rise on the back of his neck. The Mephistophelean deal with Fayed allowed no room for error. The wily Arab had stacked the deck in his favor and with no risk of exposing himself. He wondered if this was the worst deal of his life. Cold sweat soaked his shirt and the pungent odor of fear seeped from his body. He slipped a paper from his pocket and studied the numbers. He memorized them so there would be no physical trace to the account. When he was certain he knew it backwards and forwards, he tore the paper in miniscule bits. He lowered the window and watched as they flew behind the speeding car to swirl into the dessert air before floating like arid snowflakes onto the sand by the side of the road.

By the time he arrived at Quincy House, the U.S. Embassy in Riyadh, he had regained his composure. Brushing a light coat of dessert dust from his clothes, he looked up at the mansion before entering. Forsyth introduced himself at reception and was directed to follow an assistant into the Ambassador's conference room where various parties to the negotiated trade agreement waited. After apologizing for his tardiness, he took the vacant seat to the right of the Ambassador. Picking up the pen on the large conference table, he signed the document handed him by the Saudi Minister of Trade, noting as he did so the Minister had signed before he arrived.

Ambassador Russell Chesson shook both men's hands at the conclusion of the meeting. After the Minister of Trade, Amed Ataf, and the remaining parties had been escorted from the room, Chesson commented, "Congressman Forsyth that was well done. But don't for a minute expect them to adhere to the letter on what you just signed. If it suits them at the moment, you have no problem. If it doesn't, that agreement is about as valuable as used toilet paper."

His voice laced with instant anger, Forsyth snapped, "That's a cynical point of view, don't you think, Mr. Ambassador? I have always found them to be highly ethical. I thought you were assigned here because of your rapport and past dealings with the Saudis."

"My point exactly." Chesson had no use for the tight-assed Representative. He had seen men like him come and go during his forty years of service in various stations, and most of them not glamorous ones like Paris, London, and Rome. He could smell a power-hungry politician a mile away. They were most often the ones that made diplomatic service a nightmare. He didn't ask why the Speaker had felt the need to drive to Jeddah after landing rather than coming directly to the Embassy. Thinking of his friend Gerald Williams, he decided it was time they caught up with one another. As soon as this stuffy prick flew out, he would be on the phone. It was easy to drop casual comments into a conversation. Like dropping stones in a well, you waited to see if there would be any echo.

*****

Quint stared at his computer screen. The minute the image registered he hit print and waited for the sheet of paper to slip out. This message was in the same numerical code as the first: *2419.208.222.201.207.182.142.71.238.174.*1728.233.243.1512.21.3 3.36.14.52.84.*102.41.11.1728.233.243.1512.21.33.36.14.52.84.*102. 41.11.*134.172.47.195.205.*246.244.181.241.2412.*1625.91.2416.20 2.196.*231.221.199.104..133.45.1510.165.167.169.*241.*101.*81.51. 312.2312.83.188.241.*232.208.223.244.198.*227.101.2410.*147.141. 1510.2414.*2420.1519.1510.244.2315.*517.*36.*241.244.720.207.24 20.235.2425..196.164.231.2425..

He ran it through his computer program and again came up blank. He tried adding "Tony the Tiger" plus the code. Nothing popped up. Laying the first code beside the new one, he began to look for repeated patterns. The lack of real repetition in certain frequently used letters such as 'e' or 't' convinced him that the code was tied to some text and the encoder was using a random choice of picks for the various letters in order to make the messages more secure. '1510' was used once in the first message but three times in this one. Possibly this popped up more frequently as it was a letter used only once in the coding text; thus the necessity for repetition. He jotted down the English letters typically used less than one percent of the time in order of frequency.   They were 'V,' followed by 'K,' 'J,' 'X,' 'Q,' and 'Z.' As the most frequently used in the group, he put a tentative 'V' beside '1510.'   Each time used it was in the third space between double periods or a period and asterisk that he assumed meant the start and end of a word. Next he jotted down words with 'v' in the third spot and no longer than six letters since none, of what he assumed were words with 'v' in the third spot, exceeded that number. A quick list gave him 'advent, adverb, advice, anvil, advise, invite, revert, revise, seven, three, dive, five, give, hive, jive, life, live, love, rove.'   He then crossed out 'advent, adverb, invite, and anvil.' He figured 'give, hive, jive, love, and rove' were the least likely, leaving him with 'advice, advise, revert, revise, seven, dive, five, and live.' Considering this was from a terrorist cell he further culled the list to the most likely and arrived at 'advise, revise, seven, five, and live." That left him with three six-letter words with the 'V,' and two four-letter words. If the message was giving times for attacks or some event, then 'seven' was a possibility and 'five' seemed more likely than 'live.' That left him with four words: 'seven, five, advise, and revise.'

Quint checked his watch to see if he dared risk another call to Gerald to see if anyone on that side of the pond was making any headway. Noting the time was after nine in the evening in Washington, he decided to wait. There really was nothing for him to report and if Gerald learned anything, he trusted him to let him know. It was late, after two in the morning, and he was tired. Quint went to bed missing both Lila and Code. They were now the only ones left that he had any real attachment to and any feelings he had for Lila he needed to fight.

He slept late the next morning. Rising from a tumbled bed, he quickly donned his jogging clothes. Before he left for his morning run in Kensington Park, he took the precaution of hiding any papers or identifying items beneath the closet carpet that he had loosened in order to make a pocket beneath. Despite being happy with the new hotel and greater proximity to a park, he was unsure how much longer he dared trust the security of the location. The jogging path was slippery from a light drizzle and the run took longer than the thirty minutes he usually allowed. When he returned to the hotel, the paused in the lobby to purchase a newspaper and to ask the concierge to prepare his bill for the following day.

He had not placed the trip wire that he generally installed, as he wanted maid service on his room. The maid had come as both the bed and bathroom were cleaned. He glanced around to make sure that nothing else had been disturbed. The computer monitor was on and blinking. He was certain he had left the laptop turned off and unplugged. Not only was it plugged in. Someone had turned it on. He did not worry that anyone had gotten in as it was well protected by a series of codes that had to be accessed in the correct order. What concerned him was the fact that someone would have tried. He doubted it was the maid. He had met her. She was a simple country girl from Yorkshire and was totally ignorant about politics and about anything else of substance. He did not think it was an act, but he could not be sure. Quickly he searched for another hotel. That done he took his oldest shirt, a set of underwear and a pair of trousers and put them in the closet. On the desk he left a newspaper, some change, and a candy bar.

Quint's hiding place in the closet was as he left it. Quickly removing the papers he had placed there, he stowed them in his briefcase before completing the rest of his packing. After that he made the subtle alterations for his appearance to match the new passport and credit card he would use at the next hotel. Checking to be sure that he had forgotten nothing, he then began to wipe everything down. If they had already checked his room it might be wasted effort, but he would do it anyway. He carried his bags to the door and glanced around for a final check.

On a sudden inspiration, he turned back and started looking for bugging devices. Crawling around under his desk he found one glued into the corner. From there he did a thorough search and found two more. There was no question someone had tracked him. He then checked his luggage and computer bag for a bug or tracking device. Neatly concealed in the bottom of the computer case he found a tiny GPS locator. He stared at it, wondering how long he had been carrying it around and who had planted it, before flushing it down the toilet. He chuckled to himself. He hoped they would try following that one. He didn't bother to wipe down the room a second time. Hanging a 'do not disturb' sign on the outside latch, he pulled the door to behind him, careful to keep it from banging.

Not knowing if an assassin was on the way, he looked both ways when he left the room keeping his right hand on his gun. When he reached the elevator, a sudden red spot on the wall warned him he was being targeted. The gunman fired and the bullet lodged in the wall just past his head as he was already dropping to the floor. Rolling to the side, he whipped the Glock with attached silencer in the direction of the gunman and fired. A sharp yelp assured him he had hit the son of a bitch. Keeping his gun ready, he slowly crept forward to the corner of the hall where the gunman had waited for him. A trail of blood led toward the stair entrance. Quint boarded the elevator and pushed the button for the main level. He was relieved to reach the lobby and find it empty.

He was further relieved when the taxi pulled away from the curbing. Fearing the killer might be tailing him he ordered the taxi to Paddington Station, then back to Kensington while he kept an eye on the traffic. The taxi driver's glance in the rear view mirror assured Quint the man thought he was nuts. "I'm sorry for the confusion. My mother just died and I can't think straight. Take me to the Delta departure terminal at Heathrow please."

Shit, Quint thought. That was a damned piss poor excuse if he had ever heard one. On top of that the taxi driver would now remember him if questioned. Cursing steadily under his breath, he endured the heavy traffic that delayed the trip. He paid the taxi driver and entered the terminal. There he bought a ticket to Rome and paid using his own credit card and passport. Once he had the ticket he walked to the coffee bar, and ordered a coffee. Wearing a rain hat and coat, with the hat brim to shield his face and his collar turned up, he was careful to keep his face from view of the security cameras as he studied the people around him. They all seemed to be either business or tourist travelers. When he finished his coffee, he gathered his things and rented a locker to stash his guns. He then made his way to the gate for Rome. At the gate, he picked a scruffy looking teen with a backpack and tucked the credit card with a preloaded dollar amount into it while the guy looked the other way at a passing girl. He had a feeling the guy would enjoy

Rome a lot more with his little gift. Quint casually picked up his bag, returned to the locker to retrieve the satchel, and then walked to baggage claim. There he merged with the other passengers queuing up for a taxi. Red herring accomplished. If they tracked him, he hoped they would go to Rome.

"Crowe Plaza Hotel Heathrow, please."

"I don't want to lose a fare, sir, but you should know they have a shuttle that comes regularly if you want to wait for it."

"I'm on an expense account, so this is fine."

"Righto."

In the hotel, he used a passport in the name of Adam Jenkins and matching credit card to book a room on the third floor. Glancing around the lobby, he was satisfied with his choice. This location had a number of factors going for it. Businessmen and travelers frequented the large hotel. There were conference areas for hosting conventions and meetings which he would not be using. It was close to trains, air connections and rental cars. Behind the hotel there was a green area, while not as nice for jogging as the previous hotel it would have to do. The hotel also housed a spa and gym, three restaurants, pool, and bars. When Quint reached his room, he dropped his bags, locked his door and did a quick reconnaissance of the hotel to locate stairs, exits, etc. Satisfied that he was familiar with escape routes if he needed one, he returned to his room and unpacked. He was growing tired of the running routine and getting shot at. Setting up his computer he emailed Gerald to send him the number of another throwaway phone ASAP so he could call him.

*****

Royal Garden Hotel was in a panic. One of the maids called management to report the dead body of another maid in the room she had entered for cleaning. Roger Jamison, hotel manager, had dashed up to the room in panic to calm the hysterical woman. He ordered her to gather her things and move on to the next room, keeping what she had found quiet. Then he stood outside the door as he waited for the police to arrive. Roger could not imagine why someone would have murdered Sally Hicks. She was one of the sweetest and most efficient maids in his employ. His heart was heavy. He wondered if it were some kind of sex crime, but he could not go back to look. He had been warned by the police to stay out of the room and keep it secure until they could get there. In the hall he noted drops of blood leading to the stairwell and a bullet hole in the wall by the elevator. He made a note to point that out to police.

With the recent rise in crimes from the refugees that continued to flood into England, Roger like many other Brits was becoming fed up with the open-door policy that allowed the influx. Along with robbery, sex crimes were steadily increasing in frequency. He had begun to hate the Arab immigrants that caused it. In the beginning he had felt pity and a sense of doing his Christian duty by welcoming those less fortunate. He no longer felt such charity. He tried to remember which Arabs were working today's shift. He would be sure to turn their names over to the police as a precaution.

Chapter 7

"What's up man?"

"I need to keep this fast, Gerald. I don't know whom, but someone has been tracking me and I am assuming it's not the CIA or you would know where I am. I screwed up and used my old phone to call the States one time. Maybe the call was traced to my first hotel and they have been watching me ever since. I also found a bug in my briefcase. That could be how they did it. I don't know if it was just planted or if it has been there awhile. My hotel room was bugged while I was out running and some dickhead just took a shot at me. I fired back and hit him, but I have no idea how badly as he got away. I've moved but who knows how long I can stay a jump ahead of whoever is out to get me. If they come for me, I'll do my damn best to kill before I'm killed. I may need you guys to clean it up for me." Quint winced at the sound of a police siren on the road behind the hotel. The unique to Europe up and down sing-song noise was enough to announce he was out of the country.

"We can bring you in. Put you in a safe house where you can work without worrying about these bastards getting to you."

Quint snorted, "Fat chance. There is a fucking leak at the Agency, so how will I be safer?"

Ignoring the question, Gerald asked, "Anything yet on cracking the code?"

"I'm working on it." Quint checked his watch, "Time to go before your guys pick this call up on their tracker."

"Wait..." Gerald began, but Quint was already gone. Gerald swore before he smashed his phone and tossed it into the Potomac. The pressure was on at the Agency to get the code cracked. So far Jeffrey had come up with nothing. Quint was their best chance, if he could stay alive long enough to do it. Whipping another throwaway phone from his pocket, he called MI-6 in London. At the rate he was buying phones he was going to blow his office slush fund in no time.

Sidney Murchison picked up on the first ring. Gerald and Sidney had worked together on numerous cases in the Middle East. A couple of times they had saved one another's lives. He trusted the man without question. "Sid, Gerald here. I need a big one, man. I've got a guy that's trying to crack this code you emailed me. I don't know where he is for sure, but judging by his call, I'm thinking Europe and most likely the UK. His life is in danger. The hotel room he was staying in was just bugged and he was shot at. He hit the shooter who got away, and then my man did a runner. I don't know where he is now anymore than where his last hotel was."

"London is a big city. How do you suggest we go about finding this needle in a haystack." Sid leaned back and propped his feet on his desk. He had been watching the news when the phone rang but had muted the Telly to take the call. The closed caption on the screen read "Maid found murdered in Kensington hotel this morning. Authorities have no leads at the moment on motive or killer. Hotel management is puzzled. They say the young woman was a pleasant, efficient girl from Yorkshire with no known enemies."

Playing a hunch, Sid said, "Send your guy a message. Mention the murder of a maid in the Royal Garden Hotel in

Kensington this morning. See if he was staying there. There may be no connection, but if he was I'll nose around and see what I can learn."

"I'm on it. I'll get back to you as soon as I can get hold of him."

Gerald emailed Quint and waited for the phone to ring. He was tossing sticks into the river when the vibration of the phone pulled him back from his thoughts. "Quint, I need to know if you were staying at the Royal Garden Hotel in Kensington."

"Why?"

"Because they found the body of a maid in one of the rooms there this morning. There may be no connection, but..."

"Fuck!" Quint swore. "Yes, that's where my room was bugged. I cleared out right afterwards."

"Listen, I'm going to give you the name and number of a guy with MI-6 in London. He's straight arrow. You need to allow either our guys or theirs to help. If you need someone, for God's sake don't try to go it alone. These bastards aren't playing games."

"Let's have it." Quint wrote the name and number on a piece of paper after tearing it from the hotel-freebie notepad to avoid leaving an indentation on the pages beneath.

"Time's up. Gotta go."

Leaving his room, Quint hurried down to the lobby where he was just in time to catch the shuttle to the airport. At the airport, he stood in the taxi queue. When the fourth car in the line pulled up, he jumped in and told the driver to take him to a department store. While the driver waited, Quint rushed in and snatched the items he wanted, paid and returned to the taxi.

"The Ivanhoe Suite Hotel at St. Christopher's Place, please."

He checked into the hotel under the name Leonard White, the same as at the Kensington Hotel. From the Ivanhoe, he took another taxi to the Regency Hotel at Nottingham Place and again registered this time under Adam Jenkins. At the Thanet Hotel near Covent Garden, he registered under the name he had used at the Millennium, William Reynolds. All of the hotels were inexpensive and he had taken them for only one week. In each one he left clothes and a few other items to indicate he was in residence and he left a 'do not disturb' sign on each door. Hopefully he had created enough confusion to buy a little time. Returning to the airport, he again took the shuttle back to the hotel.

He snagged a paper on his way through the lobby glancing at it on the way to his room. The big news was the Queen's appearance at Parliament at noon the next day, October third. Quint read the article through and then reread it. It bothered him. If terrorists wanted to make some kind of grand statement, this was the perfect opportunity to take out not only the Queen, but ruling members of the government as well. Such an event would send the world reeling into shock.

Picking up the messages he went to work on them. With ten letters in Parliament, he began checking both messages for a word with ten letters. He found it in the second message. Of the two messages, this was the longest word in either. He started counting letters: 'London' six, 'noon' four, 'Parliament' ten, 'October' seven, and 'three' with five letters. Going to the second message he counted the letters for the spaces between '*.'

If he inserted the words: 'London. Noon. Parliament., ???, Three.' He screwed his mouth as he stared at the fourth word with only three letters. If October were shortened to 'Oct.,' it would fit. It was guesswork, but it made sense. Picking up the phone he called the number Gerald had given him.

"Sidney Murchison, here."

"Sidney, you don't know me but Gerald Williams told me I could call you."

"Ah, you're the code breaker, Quinton Cord, isn't it?"

"Yes."

"What may I do for you, Quinton?"

"What would you say if I told you terrorists are planning something major at the Parliament building tomorrow when the Queen is there?"

"What makes you say that?" Sidney sat up in his chair, holding his breath as he awaited the reply.

"I can't prove it, but I've been working on this coded message and it seems to fit with the meeting tomorrow. That is the only part I can take a stab at, as I still haven't figured out the document the numbers are taken from. I thought you should be on the alert just in case."

"Have you run this by Gerald?"

"Not yet. I want to crack more of this to see if there is anything planned stateside first."

"Security has already swept the building and established control. I'll let them know to do another sweep. Thanks for the heads up."

Quint hung up and sat staring at the computer screen. He had already made a number of guesses that seemed to fit. Why not make some more? He picked up the messages and noted that none of the numbers exceeded 24 if the first two numbers were paired. If the second row of numbers were paired none exceed 32. Taken singly no first number exceeded 9, and no second number exceeded 9 leading him to believe the numbers in the code were paired. He postulated that the first number or pair referred to the particular line in the source, and the second or third number or pair the position in the line of a particular letter. If these assumptions were correct, then the text would have to be either a quote or perhaps a poem that was 24 lines long and with relatively short lines. A poem seemed the likely bet. The next step was to find a poem with 24 lines that made reference to a tiger.

When he did a search only one poem popped up: The Tyger by William Blake. Hitting print, he soon held the poem in his hand:

THE TYGER

By William Blake

Tyger! Tyger! burning bright
In the forests of the night,
What immortal hand or eye
Could frame thy fearful symmetry?
In what distant deeps or skies
Burnt the fire of thine eyes?
On what wings dare he aspire?
What the hand dare sieze the fire?
And what shoulder, & what art.
Could twist the sinews of thy heart?
And when thy heart began to beat,
What dread hand? & what dread feet?
What the hammer? what the chain?
In what furnace was thy brain?

What the anvil? what dread grasp
Dare its deadly terrors clasp?
When the stars threw down their spears,
And watered heaven with their tears,
Did he smile his work to see?
Did he who made the Lamb make thee?
Tyger! Tyger! burning bright
In the forests of the night,
What immortal hand or eye
Dare frame thy fearful symmetry?

Using that as the key, he numbered the lines and at the end of each line wrote in the number of letters in the line. Quint picked up the first message and translated it. It read: **'D.C. set. London waiting for schedule. Problems Paris. Will advise.'**

Excited with the success, he hurried to translate the second message: **'London, Noon, Parliament. Oct. three. Ready Paris, will advise date location. D.C. Willard Hotel, seven pm, Oct. five. Deposit sent'.**

He called Sid to give him the key to the code and the two translated messages. It was up to the British to take care of the situation at Parliament. Next he sent the email to Gerald letting him know to call him ASAP. While he waited he scrolled through the websites to see if there was any chatter on the terrorist sites about events scheduled in Paris and Washington. It was of tantamount importance that the perpetrators stay ignorant of the fact the code was now compromised in order to receive future transmissions. It was up to the computer spooks in Washington or Lila to track down the origin of the coded messages in order to get to the guy pulling the strings. Quint wanted to get the bastard himself but Langley would tell him it was beyond his pay-grade and abilities...but then they didn't know his abilities beyond code breaking.   While it might be beyond what he was commissioned to do, the need for personal revenge for his caretakers' deaths ate at him.   Hopefully they could stop any plans for destruction in Parliament or at the Willard.   As for Paris, they would have to await another message.

Quint got up the next morning and stared out his window at the steady rain.   The gloom matched his mood.   If the British had not found the means of destruction planned for noon at the Parliament building, it could be catastrophic.   Not only the Queen and the Prime Minister would be there, but both houses of Parliament as well.   Too restless to sit still and watch events unfold on the live news feed, he dressed carefully assuming an entirely different persona.   Satisfied with the older man that stared back at him from the mirror, he slipped his Glock and silencer into one pocket of his raincoat and extra clips in the other.   He was going to Parliament.   Again he rode the shuttle to the airport taxi queue and from there took a taxi downtown.   Ever cautious, on the edge of central London he switched to the tube for the final leg of the trip.   When he climbed up to street level, he unfurled his umbrella and tugged the hat brim lower over his face.   With a newspaper under his arm, he looked like countless other commuters on their way to work.

His phone rang just as he reached the street.   Walking around the corner and facing into a solid stone wall, he answered, "Gerald.   I cracked the code.   They are using the William Blake poem 'The Tyger.'   These assholes are planning something for the meeting at the Parliament here in London.   I warned Sidney at MI-6 and the Brits are getting right on it. They also plan something for Washington when POTUS and the Veep are doing a fund raiser at the Willard."

"Yes. I am aware of the Willard dinner. I'll get our guys on it ASAP."

"Don't let on to the Agency we know the code until you catch the mole. I want to see what else they are up to and I don't want them to realize we are on to them. They're going after Paris, too, but they don't yet have the details posted. Whoever is behind this is one serious mother-fucker."

"You are right on all counts, brother. I will probably get my ass in the wringer with my boss, but until I know the leak in the Agency, I will give a quiet heads-up to a friend of mine in the FBI and the President's Security detail." Gerald paused to toss his cigarette out the car window, "Thanks, Quint. You do good work. In the meantime, I can handle this. You need to get somewhere safe and lay low until we catch the asshole."

"I'll do my best," Quint replied. Slipping the phone into his pocket, he casually glanced around before merging with a group just leaving the tube station. He walked with them until he reached the corner, where he turned and continued on his way.

After hanging up with Quint, Gerald used the same phone to call Buster Walton and clue him in. Not only would Gerald leak the intelligence to the FBI and the President's security detail, but he also wanted Buster to go after the perps. Less constrained by rules and regulations than the government agencies that secretly hired him, Buster would do whatever it took to discover the mastermind behind the planned attacks. After he detailed what he knew, Gerald asked, "Do you know if

Jeffrey had any luck tracking the origin of these messages?"

"When I talked to him an hour ago, he was working on it. He was also spending time trying to crack the code. Now that your guy has done that, Jeffrey can concentrate on the source point. I'll call and get him on that exclusively. Watch your backs until we can catch this prick."

"Will do."

Gerald checked the jamming device that the Agency installed in official cars to make sure it was still workiing. He had used the phone for two calls and continuing to call on it made him nervous, but until he could stop and buy another, he needed to use it. This was too important to wait. Hopefully if someone were trying to pick him up, the jammer would provide necessary interference. After hanging up with Richard Norris in the FBI office, he next called Fred Massey with the security detail to fill him in on what he knew. Both men could be trusted to keep his name out of it. On the way to his office, he stopped and bought three more time-loaded phones. The next stop was the dead-end off Turkey Loop Road that he used for making the previous calls. Leaving his car running, he walked to within throwing distance of the Potomac River and pitched the used phone in.

When he reached his office, Marlowe Hollins was not at her desk. Walking into his office, he found her leaning over his computer. "What's up, Mrs. Hollins?"

He watched a blush suffuse her face with color, "Did you need something from my computer?"

"Oh, no. I was looking for a file on your desk and brushed against it. I was just checking I had not messed anything up."

"I'm sure it's fine. Now if you'll excuse me, I need to get

busy. Unless you need something, just close the door on your way out." Gerald nodded dismissively. His antenna was up. Surely it was nothing, but he needed to be sure. He tapped his pencil in a steady rhythm as he stared at the closed door thinking hard. If anyone had access to his files she did. Twice now he had caught her nosing around his office when he was out. Perhaps, he needed to add some cheese to the mousetrap to see if she came to nibble. Still puzzled as to what she was up to, he started going through his emails. Midway down the mail file he found one from an unidentified source. When he opened it, a shiver ran down his spine. Someone nasty knew that he was leading the investigation into the mystery code. Picking up his phone, he called the Director.

"Mr. Thomas, if you aren't busy, I need to talk."

"Now why would I be busy? I don't do anything around here, you know," Thomas snarled.

Gerald winced and swallowed a curse, "Sorry, sir. That was a dumb remark. It's urgent or I would not have bothered you."

"Alright. I can see you in five minutes if you make it fast. I have another appointment shortly."

"I'll be there."

Gerald looked down at the pencil he was holding. He had broken another one in half. He swore, 'Fuck it. Why do I let that pecker-head rile me up?'

He paused at Marlowe's desk on the way to the Director's office, "Mrs. Hollins, I will be with the Mr. Thomas if you need me. I won't be long."

She glanced up and smiled, "No problem."

Chapter 8

He sat chewing on his hamburger at the terrace cafe on the first floor of the building, not tasting it...although it was a favorite. Typically he would have walked for a mile or so afterwards, but today he decided to skip it. If he were threatened, perhaps his family was as well. Pondering it as he walked back to his office, he decided better safe than sorry. Under the circumstances, he couldn't much blame Quint for running.

Knowing that Jill preferred a text message rather than phone calls when she was working on a painting, he sent her a message telling her to pack the kids and head for her parent's cottage in Chesapeake Estates on Kent Island that afternoon and to tell no one. He would call her later and explain. He would have preferred to explain in person and see them off, but he had several memos he had to send out before he could leave for the day. As it was, he expected it would be hours before he could call it a day.

An hour later Jill rolled back the sunroof on the car, turned on the classical music channel, and checked the kids in the rear view mirror. Both were nodding off, promising a peaceful drive. Code was sitting tall and proud in the passenger seat. Despite her initial trepidation about having the dog join their household, she was enjoying him. She suspected the animal of waging a charm campaign against her. Smiling to herself, she anticipated the weekend ahead. Gerald had a habit of planning something special for their anniversary. Sunday would be their fifth. They did not have an elaborate lifestyle since she was a stay at home mom. While her paintings earned money from time to time, she had to accept they would never make any real income with just a civil servant's salary. Gerald and she didn't mind about the income as long as their family was provided with a decent life.

It was just over an hour's drive to Kent Island, noted for its rustic rural feel and limited shopping. She knew from experience to stop in Annapolis to buy what they would need for a few days at the cottage. Located on Bay Drive at almost the south end of the historic island, their cottage was little more than a revamped farmhouse. It was perhaps fifty yards from the water and surrounded on the other sides by pastureland and forest. Although her parents rarely used it, Chester Norris checked on it periodically and let them know if anything was amiss. As the nearest neighbor, Chester kept some cattle in their pasture in repayment for keeping an eye on things. In his sixties and widowed, the cattle was more a time filler than any real enterprise. With the children resettled in the car along with groceries and some basic staples, she called Chester on her cell phone to let him know she was on the way. She could count on him to go to the house, turn on the hot water, and have it ready for her when she arrived.

Gerald called that night after the children were in bed. He sounded so tired and upset that she was instantly alarmed. After he told her why he had asked her to leave town so precipitously, she was even more alarmed. And when he told her to get down the sawed off double barrel H&R 12-gauge shotgun and load it, and to do the same with the Walther PPQ pistol, she was downright scared.

"Honey, for goodness sake, what on earth is going on?"

"Jill, you know I can't discuss office business. I am probably just being overly cautious anyway. But, until I have some serious answers to some tough questions, I would just rather my family were out of town. I'll come for the weekend. You know I wouldn't miss an anniversary with my favorite girl."

They talked for another five minutes before ringing off. Jill wasted no time loading the guns and then checking all of the doors and windows to make sure they were secure. Code followed her around like it was a tour of duty. Remembering he was a trained police dog, she supposed it was. Jill was glad to have his comforting presence in the house. Although Gerald had not mentioned it, tomorrow she would have Chester do a once over on the powerful Sea-Ray they kept in the boathouse when they were away...just in case. She decided it might not be a bad idea to park the car close to the house and positioned so there was no need to back up to leave. Once that was finished, she would try to enjoy the time with her children while she waited for Gerald to arrive.

*****

Gerald was sound asleep when a noise that did not belong in the night awoke him. He lay still listening. The noise sounded again from the rear of the house. Grabbing a loaded Para Black Ops Combat 45 from the nightstand, he cautiously began to descend the backstairs. When he reached the kitchen, he could see the silhouette of a man back-lit by moonlight. Gerald watched as the man on the other side of the glass cut a circle in the door window and carefully removed a section of glass. He then reached in and fumbled with the lock. Gerald chuckled as he watched the futile effort. As the man started to extract his hand, Gerald clamped down on it and fired a shot hitting his shoulder. Keeping a grip on the hand, he hissed, "Drop the gun or you're a dead man."

"Fuck you."   He could tell by the accent the man was Eastern European.

"Sorry, you stupid bastard.   This time you're the one fucked."   Knocking the rest of the glass from the window with the pistol, he shot the guy in both knees. Screaming in agony the man hit the ground like a dead tree.   Even though the shoulder shot had somewhat incapacitated the man's right hand, he took out some insurance by putting another bullet through the left hand. The gun that had dropped when he shot him in the shoulder was useless to the man now.

Gerald unlocked the door and dragged him into the kitchen before kicking the thug's gun into the yard. He would retrieve it later. "Who are you?"

"Fuck you."

"Wrong answer, asshole." Gerald found himself reverting to the field agent mode that got results by any means necessary. Stomping viciously on the shattered left kneecap, he asked again, "I'm out of patience, you fucker. Who are you and why are you trying to break into my home?"

Writhing in pain, the man muttered, "Abdul."

"Who're you working for?"

"I don't know," Abdul panted.

"You ought to know better than to lie to me by now." This time Gerald stomped on his right kneecap. The sudden pain sent the man into unconsciousness. While he waited for him to come around, he called Buster to tell him to haul ass to his house and come to the back door.

Buster didn't ask why. "On my way. Probably be twenty minutes. You okay?"

"Yeah."

Gerald was sitting at the kitchen counter watching the man bleed on his floor when his friend arrived. Buster stepped over broken glass and walked in. He looked at the man on the floor and the gun in Gerald's hand. He didn't need anyone to draw a map to read the situation.

"Damn, man. You must have really been pissed to shoot him four times."

"Somebody hired this piece of shit to come here and harm me and my family, so yeah, I'm pissed."

"Where are Jill and the kids? They must be scared stiff with all this ruckus."

"Got a tip an asshole might be dropping by. I had them pack up and leave this afternoon, thank God."

"Damn."

"Buster, I need you to take this fucker somewhere real private. See if you can find out who hired him. You know what to do after that. I'm keeping this one between us. Until I can plug the leak, I'm not telling the Agency shit."

"No problem. Help me get him wrapped up in something so he doesn't mess up my car. Might be a good idea if you help carry him, too. He ain't walking anywhere in that condition."

Abdul's eyes blinked open as both men stared at him. "Well, it looks like the piss-ant is waking up. I'll be right back with a shower curtain and a blanket. Keep an eye on the bastard for me."

Gerald returned with the items and laid the shower curtain on the floor and then spread the blanket over it. Both men then rolled the Arab onto the covering and wrapped him up like a cocoon using cord to keep it in place. Abdul whimpered in pain and passed out again while they worked.

"Buster snorted, "He looks like a turd in a bun."

Gerald glanced down and grinned, "He does at that. By the way, do you have some painkiller left at the shack? If so, dole out just enough to keep him talking."

"Yeah. And don't worry, if he knows anything I'll get it out of him." Buster stood back and looked at their handiwork. "Get his feet and I'll take his shoulders. We'll put him in the trunk."

"Right. Do you have anyone to help you when you get him there." Gerald knew the shack Buster used for situations like this was in the woods in Maryland. The location was remote, and perfect for clandestine purposes. It wasn't the first time Gerald had called Buster to take some guy there that he wanted interrogated without having to worry about government guidelines and congressional inquiries.

"I called a couple of my men on the way here and put them on stand by. Soon as we get this sack of shit loaded, I'll call them and tell them to meet me. They'll be at the shack before I am."

"Good. When you're finished with him, he needs to disappear completely."

"Will do." Buster slapped Gerald on the back. "You might want to take a little vacation with your family for a few days until we can get a lead on this."

"I intend to do just that." Gerald reached into the drawer where he kept his things and pulled out a secure phone. "Use this to call me. My number is already programmed in. Just don't call the usual cell number or my office phone. I suspect they may be tapped."

Buster chuckled, "You got yourself in some deep shit for a desk jockey."

"Yeah and between us if that asshole Thomas gives me much more shit, he can stick this job where the sun don't shine."

"I told you to quit the bastard. You can make a hell of a lot more in business with me. I could use you. We were quite a team, remember?"

"For sure we were. And thanks for the offer. That's good to have on the back burner." Gerald glanced at his friend and then at the trussed up man on the floor. "I owe you one for this."

"Forget it. You've done me plenty of favors."

By the time Gerald finished mopping the floor with disinfectant and running the washer with plenty of Clorox to destroy any DNA left in the rags, the sun was just beginning to rise. He retrieved the gun from the backyard, dropped it into a plastic baggy, and put it the drawer at the desk Jill called her recipe desk. He decided there was no point in going back to bed. He was too keyed up to sleep. He showered, dressed, and had his bag packed, and was in the car in less than twenty minutes. It was not a bad idea to be out of town should another hired gun decide to drop in. Once he was in the car, he used his Langley issued cell phone to call Marshall Thomas and report the attempted break-in.

"Mr. Thomas, sorry to bother you so early on a Saturday morning, but I thought you should know the warning email I got meant business. Someone tried to break into my house last night."

"Did you get the guy?"

Gerald lied, "No, he got away, but I think it would be a good idea to take my family and leave town for a few days. I will keep working remote and if I learn anything I'll let you know."

"I've got an uneasy feeling on this code business. My gut tells me something big is about to happen. How much longer before Cord cracks the damned thing?"

"All I know is he is working on it. As soon as he gets it translated, I'll let you know," again he lied. "In the meantime, I need you to have someone run a check on Marlowe Hollins. She's making me a little uneasy with the snooping around my files and computer. I'm beginning to wonder if she's the mole. I left a file on my desk marked top secret. It's wiped clean of prints. If she picks it up, you can have it dusted and something should show up. Inside I created a red herring. I said that Quint was holed up at the Marriott in Alexandria and that he thought he was making progress on the code. I already have Adam Russell checking on that if someone shows up looking for him."

"Good, I'll follow up with Adam and put a couple of our guys in your house as well."

"Do you need me to drop a key off somewhere?"

"Come on, we're better than that. It would save time if you gave me the security code though."

Gerald gave it to him. He added, "I have the perp's gun. I left it in the desk drawer in the kitchen. Our man can get it so someone can run a check for fingerprints. The guy was wearing gloves so that's unlikely, but a trace on the weapon might tell us something."

After they hung up, Gerald looked at the phone in amazement. Thomas had actually been civil despite the early hour.

Taking no chances on being followed, Gerald looped around the streets of Washington for over an hour. When he picked up no tail, he wove his way through traffic to head to a shopping center on the outskirts of town where a jeweler was holding the anniversary gift for his wife. Glancing at his watch, he saw that he still had over an hour to kill before the store opened. Pulling into a Starbucks, he went inside grabbed a newspaper, cup of cappuccino, and a scone. A banquette was empty on the back wall and he made his way to it, settling in so he could watch the door like any good Chicago gangster. He kept his eye on the wall clock. It would take him less than five minutes to reach the Jewelry store. As a freestanding unit it opened at nine rather than opening at ten like the rest of the mall. He planned to walk in the minute it opened and then head to Kent Island. When he finished the last of the cappuccino, he laid the newspaper to one side and used his secure phone to call his wife to let her know he was on the way. He read the relief in her voice and sensed that her night had held little more sleep than his.

"What say we take a nap when we put the kids down for theirs?"

"Gerald Williams, I know you well enough to translate that one. And, the answer is yes...then a nap!"

Gerald was grinning like a teenager when he clicked off his phone. In minutes he had his gift and was ready to leave town. He had just turned onto Route 50 when his phone rang again. That nap would have to wait.

Chapter 9

Quint watched the line waiting at St. Stephen's Gate. The line had formed on the right for admission to the Stranger's Galleries of the House of Lords. Despite being arguably the more prestigious of the two houses, it was actually easier to gain admittance to it, rather than the line on the left leading to the House of Commons. Quint was looking for anyone that seemed nervous or out of place. He had no chance of gaining entry with a gun in his pocket. That was true of a terrorist as well. The best way to create the desired destruction seemed to him to be a bomb. Plastique with detonators was not that difficult to hide. The bomb could be set off with timers or a cell phone. The cell phone seemed the more practical since there was no guarantee that everyone would arrive on time. Surely if plastique had been hidden inside the building, dogs would have sniffed it out by now. After his call to MI-6, he felt the Brits would have gone back through with a fine-toothed comb. The terrorists would be operating on the principle that the code had not been broken and thus unaware of any efforts to thwart the plot.

Barricades kept the crowd behind lines on both sides of the street. Londoners and tourists alike were gathering for a chance to glimpse the Queen and other dignitaries. He mingled into the throng and began to pick out security agents. They were not difficult to spot the world over...the same focused scan, the same non-descript dark clothing and glasses, the same earpieces and discreet microphones, and the same bulk under the clothing indicating a weapon. Watching the growing number of spectators, he rethought the options open to the terrorists. Initially he had assumed whatever was planned would be inside the Parliament building. Rethinking the actual message he realized that it did not indicate whether it was to be inside or outside the building. What if the bomb were in a backpack or pocket-vest intended for detonation at the moment the Queen arrived? With so many people milling about jostling for a better view, security was presented with a constantly shifting scenario of possibilities.

Suddenly Quint was bumped from behind. He quickly regained balance and turned to see who had caused it. He spotted a dark-headed figure rudely working his way through the crowd to a frontal position near the ceremonial entry door. With a Leica hanging around his neck, a camera bag over one shoulder, and a tourist map protruding from the pocket of his Burberry raincoat, he looked like a tourist impatient to get a photo of the big event. Not seeing anyone that seemed more likely, Quint made a sudden decision to follow the man. Pushing through the spectators, he ignored the comments of those he nudged aside as he jockeyed his way to within an arm's length of his target where the man had positioned himself between two parked police vans.

A sudden cheer caused every head but Quint's and the man he watched to swivel in the direction of the Queen's arrival. Standing slightly behind the man who was intent on the contents of the bag slung over his shoulder, he watched to see what he was up to. He edged nearer and caught a glimpse of wired explosives in the bag. He didn't need to see more and he could not afford the time it would take to attract a policeman.

With the silencer already screwed in place, Quint put a bullet into the man's side angled to reach towards his heart. The man began to crumple as his body reacted to the trauma. Quint eased the body into a sitting position beside the van. Casually he leaned over and pretended to be talking to him as he opened the bag to see if the bomb was armed. He surveyed the spectators to see if anyone was watching him. With all eyes still on the gently waving figure of the elderly Queen, he was momentarily unobserved. Quint had studied enough bomb devices to figure out it was triggered by a cell phone. He had even made a few that he planted around his house just in case he needed some heavy discouragement of an intruder. He traced the wires until he found the one he wanted and snatched it free. Wiping the sweat from his brow, he removed the phone from the dead man's pocket and shoved it into his own before rejoining the cheering crowd. He stood for a minute cheering like the others before quietly fading into the background. He walked to the Westminster tube station, bought a ticket and took the tube as far as Charing Cross. He could not see anyone acting as though they were waiting for an explosion. That provided a margin of comfort, as there could always have been a back up bomber. Pulling out his phone once he reached the street, he called Sidney.

He wasted no time on a greeting. "There's a dead man sitting on the street between two police cars in front of Parliament. His camera bag is loaded with explosives rigged for a cell phone triggered detonation. I don't know if there are any accomplices around so it would be a real good idea to get your bomb squad on it ASAP."

"Hold it for a sec." Quint could hear Sidney relaying the

information to one of the units stationed nearby. Coming back to the call, he remarked, "I suspect I shouldn't ask how he met his end?"

"Probably not."

"Is the threat neutralized?"

"Yes, as best I could tell, although I'll feel better when that bag is out of there. And, the Queen as well." Quint looked up as a pedestrian passed. He tugged his collar up and hunched his shoulders. He was nervous. "And, Sid, I need a quick private trip home. The weather here is a little warm for me right now. Can you arrange it?"

"That shouldn't be a problem. Where are you? I'll pick you up and take you to Luton Airport where we keep a plane for these occasions."

"The Crowne Plaza Hotel at Heathrow."

"I know it. Pack up your things and wait for me in your room. I'll call you when I get to the hotel. There'll be an agency plane waiting for you in the Luton private terminal at one o'clock sharp."

Fifty minutes later Quint climbed into the passenger side of Sidney's car. Reaching over he shook his hand. "Nice to meet you face to face."

"You as well."

Quint buckled his seatbelt. "I never can get used to sitting on the left side of the car and finding no steering wheel."

"I feel the same way when I'm in the States and try to drive on the right side." Sidney turned into traffic and began the drive to Luton. As they drove, he studied the code breaker out of the corner of his eye. The man was perfect for clandestine work as he had the kind of looks and demeanor that could blend in or be easily altered to look like someone else. He thought Gerald was wasting the man's talents. Looking at the fit of his jacket it was obvious Quint worked out. He walked like a man light on his feet and alert to his surroundings.

He blurted, "Did you ever consider living on this side of the pond? I wouldn't have any trouble getting you a job in MI-6, especially after the favor you just did us."

"Aw, come on Sid. Afraid not. At least not at the moment, but I'll keep it in mind. And thanks for the offer. I won't tell Gerald you tried to turn me." Quint grinned.

Sidney chuckled, "That's bloody good of you. By the way, our bomb squad guys have the explosives. Strange thing, it seems the guy's phone went missing. Now, I don't suppose you would care to turn it over?"

"Sorry, never saw it." Quint felt no shame at the lie. After all he had just saved British Intelligence Services the embarrassment of a dead Queen along with numerous dignitaries and civilians. He didn't need a medal and he sure as hell didn't need questions about the weapon he had just used in a homicide. He wanted Lila working her computer magic to find out as much as she could before he turned the phone over to Gerald. After that Gerald could share the phone with Sid and MI-6 if he wanted to. The code was cracked, but he had no intention of being sidelined until he caught the man responsible for murdering his caretakers. It was a private vendetta. The attempts on his own life made him angry, but the murders of two people he loved caused a burn for personal vengeance on their behalf.

Sidney knew better than to push. There were other ways to get the phone. Sooner or later, Gerald would fill him in on what they knew on their end. In the meantime, MI-6 could breathe a sigh of relief. Then they would begin a serious study of how they had missed the threat in an area scanned repeatedly for days for anyone or anything suspicious. He chuckled to himself. The nerdy code-breaker appeared to have skills unsuspected by the CIA. He could hardly wait to call Gerald and tell him what had just happened and to advise him to be waiting for MI-6's 'special delivery' to Andrews Air Base.

They pulled next to a private hanger where Sidney nodded to the waiting plane. "You'll be on your way to Langley in about five minutes. I will notify Gerald you are en route and to clear the plane for landing. I suspect you need to lay low until this thing is cracked, but I have a strong hunch you won't."

Quint gave a non-committal shrug as he walked away from the car. At the top of the stairs, he waved goodbye before ducking into the plane. He was the only passenger. The door was closed and the plane rolling down the tarmac before he even got the seatbelt buckled. As he settled back, he glanced around the cabin. It was the cushiest he had ever ridden in. Pale cream-colored leather seats lined one wall with small walnut tabletops between each one. On the opposite wall was a long leather sofa. As his eyes traveled around the cabin they settled on a gorgeous brunette sitting aft. She was staring at him.

"Hello, the name is Greta," she purred. "I am here to see to your comfort. As soon as we reach altitude, I'll get you a drink and something to eat. That is unless you would rather take a nap? There is a king size bed through that door, as well as a bath with shower." She nodded her head to the door at her left.

Quint smiled at her, wondering just how much comfort she was willing to take care of. "Thanks, I'm wound a little tight right now, so a drink would be great.   Is this a regular assignment for you?"

"Oh, I do this and that. Whatever the agency needs more or less." She was an easy conversationalist and soon they were laughing and talking like old friends.   Greta asked a few questions of a personal nature that Quint chose to ignore. He wasn't in the habit of giving out details to anyone about his life and certainly not to a stranger, no matter how pleasant and blatantly sexual.

When the seatbelt sign went off, she unbuckled and walked to the galley giving him ample time to study the sway of her hips. He couldn't deny the sudden desire that rushed to his groin. Picking up a magazine he put it in his lap while he waited for the glass of champagne he had asked for.

She leaned over just enough to give him a good look down her blouse, before saying, "I'll be right back with a snack."

"Great. Why don't you join me?" At the moment Quint didn't have any objection to joining the mile high club.

"Oh, I fully plan on it." She winked before she returned to the galley for the food.

After an hour or so had passed an empty champagne bottle sat on the table between them. Standing she stretched, "Why don't you let me show you the stateroom. I'm sure you will be much more comfortable there."

Quint took the hand she extended. "That's an offer I can't refuse."

Opening the door, she gestured for him to enter, "Make yourself comfortable. I'll be back to check on you as soon as I take some food and drinks to the cockpit."

Quint dropped his clothes on the bathroom floor and

climbed into the shower. What a luxury to have a bath and a waiting bed on the six-hour flight. Thinking about Greta, he had a feeling the flight was going to seem way too short. Ten minutes later the glass on the shower was steamed so he could barely see out but there was no mistaking the nude figure that appeared on the other side of the door. Popping it open, Greta stepped in and began languorously rubbing soap over her lush body. He watched for a minute before he decided he had a better idea. Taking the soap, he took over where she left off. With the soap rinsed off, they left the shower. Standing beside it, Quint grabbed a towel and dried them both.

"Feel like having that 'nap' now?" He cocked an eyebrow at her in invitation.

"That sounds lovely, Quint." She reached for him as she said it, pleased to find him ready, "Hmm, very, very nice."

She was a voracious lover. After coming twice, he could oblige her no more. Tired and the most relaxed he had been in weeks he felt sleep creeping up on him. He turned on his side and nestled into his pillow. He had not quite fallen asleep when Greta left the bed. Opening one eye a slit, he watched as she walked over to his jacket and began riffling the pockets.

"If you'll tell me what you are looking for, maybe I could save you the trouble."

Stunned, she dropped both the terrorist's phone and his on the floor. Quint jumped from the bed and snatched them from her. "So this is the kind of thing you do for the agency?"

"Whatever." She gave him a saucy grin, "Even if I didn't get the phone, I enjoyed the tumble."

"I think you need to go back into the cabin now. See if the pilot needs a little ass with his coffee."

"Tsk, tsk. Don't be nasty. You enjoyed yourself too." She slipped through the door carrying her clothes in one hand.

Quint locked the door, before crawling back into the bed. He fell asleep in moments. He was jarred from a dream several hours later by a knocking on the door.

"Rise and shine, lover boy. We are thirty minutes from touchdown."

Quint dressed, washed his face and gathered his things. When he emerged into the cabin he was greeted with a cup of coffee and crisp hot croissant with butter and jam.

"After all that exercise I thought you might be hungry." Greta winked, "My boss will be a lot happier with me if you would give me have that phone."

"Sorry, I'm keeping my phone."

"Let's not play games. You know which one I mean."

He saw her reaching in her pocket and was instantly wary. Grabbing her wrist he jerked her hand out and tore the hypodermic needle from her hand. Jabbing it into her thigh, Quint watched as she slowly crumpled onto the sofa. He leaned over and covered her with a blanket. His voice was deadly quiet when he said, "I can't afford to play games, lady."

Thirty minutes later the pilot poked his head from the door just after the plane landed. "Home safe in the USA."

"Thanks." He nodded his head to the sleeping stewardess, "She said she's tired and is going to take a nap. I can get the door for you if you'd like?"

"Sure."

Quint glanced back. Greta was just beginning to come around. Wasting no time, he opened the door, and pushed the button that automatically lowered the steps. Grabbing his things, he climbed down to find Gerald waiting at the foot of the stairs.

"Welcome home. Sid tells me you've been a busy boy." He pointed to the waiting black SUV, "I'm taking you somewhere safe. Things have heated up around here since our last chat."

Gerald called Jill to let her know he was running late and would be bringing a houseguest. She had known him long enough to figure out something must have happened at the office and to accept another of her husband's late arrivals.

*****

Douglas Forsyth leaned back in his easy chair watching the BBC. He was expecting the news to be interrupted at any moment with the announcement of carnage in London. So far he felt confident. He had a man in Rome looking for Cord, one at the Marriott in Alexandria following up on Marlowe's tip, and five monitoring hotels in London. Another man was trying to get a fix on Gerald Williams' location. That was the only frustration. They had all vanished. The fucking code-breaker should have been long dead. If Williams and his family had been taken, he could have squeezed the man for everything he knew and then silenced him for good. His family unfortunately would have been collateral damage. Having heard nothing from Abdul, he was nervous. He hoped the dumb-assed Arab was dead and Langley had quietly dumped him. The last thing he wanted was the stupid son-of-a-bitch talking. So far Prince Fayed had supplied him with total shit for wet work.

Forsyth watched for an hour and still there was nothing but cheering crowds milling around outside Parliament. He glanced at the speech he had prepared denouncing the ISIS terrorists. If something didn't happen when the Queen left, he was fucked.   Thirty minutes later the Queen's entourage departed without a hitch.   Right after that, a reporter on the scene breathlessly announced an unknown gunman had stopped a terrorist attack.   The terrorist was killed before he could detonate a bag full of high-powered explosives.   Forsyth sat up in his chair.

"Fucking hell!   Have I got to do this shit myself?" he screamed.   He threw his glass of fifty-year old Highland Park scotch against the wall and watched as it ran down the wall to puddle around the broken glass.

His wife hurried into the room, "Did you call, honey?"

"Get your ass out of here.   I don't need to deal with you right now," he snarled.

Her face froze.   Without a word, she turned on her heel and walked from the room wondering when she had begun to hate the bastard.

Chapter 10

Quint surprised himself by the instant rapport he felt with the Williams boys, James called Jimbo and George called Georgie. When they learned that Code was his dog, there was an initial hostility quickly quelled when he told them they could each have one of Code's first puppies when he became a father. Both parents had groaned while the boys grinned with glee.

With a delicious home cooked meal under his belt, and a long day behind him, Quint was soon yawning. He could tell by the glances traded by Jill and Gerald they were ready for bed as well. Excusing himself, he stood up and volunteered to settle the boys for the night with no objections from the parents.

Quint tucked them in and listened to their prayers. For a moment he was carried back to his childhood when his mother had made it a nightly ritual. It warmed something deep inside that he had long forgotten. It was in that moment that he decided that he would someday have kids of his own to tuck in and love. It was a revelation as he had never before even considered the possibility. A woman in his life, yes...a wife and children no. He wondered if in this one evening everything could have changed. He went to the guest room, shed his clothes, and crawled beneath the covers. Code curled up on the floor next to his bed. He fell asleep with his fingers curled in Code's fur.

He was awakened by Code's low-pitched growls. The dog stood and nudged him to full awareness. Quint listened to see what had alarmed the dog, but could hear nothing beyond the typically night sounds of the countryside. He trusted Code. The animal was too intelligent and well trained to have awakened him for nothing. He sprang from the bed, snatched on his pants and grabbed his gun, checking to be sure it was fully loaded. Code followed him to the Williams' bedroom where he knocked on the door and plunged in without waiting for an invitation. Both Gerald and Jill sat up in bed in surprise. He was embarrassed when he realized they had not been asleep but enjoying a private time together. Judging by the hastily grabbed covers they were even more embarrassed as they struggled to hide their nudity.

Putting that from his mind, he said, "Something's going down. Code just woke me up. I learned a long time ago not to ignore him. Jill, go to the boys' room, put them in the bathtub, get in with them and pull one of their twin mattresses over y'all. Gerald get your gun and come with me."

Gerald was momentarily stunned at this nerdy code-breaker's instant command of the situation, but now was no time to question it. He climbed from the bed and snatched his trousers from the floor. He zipped them up and then tossed Jill a robe. "Do what he says, honey! And, try not to worry. We're on it."

Jill waited for them to leave before grabbing the robe and running to her sons' room. Tossing towels and pillows in the tub to make it more comfortable, she lifted the sleeping children and carried them one by one to the tub. They didn't even awaken. She then snatched a blanket from their bed, tossed it through the bathroom door, and dragged in a mattress from the crib that still stood in the corner. Locking the door behind her, she tucked the blanket around her sons and pushed the mattress over them. For several minutes she sat on the floor by the tub. There was no way she could just crawl in and wait, not with every nerve ending screaming for her to do something. It wasn't that she didn't trust the men to protect them...she wanted to help. Leaving the boys, she inched from the bathroom and dashed back to the master bedroom where she grabbed the shotgun and pistol she had loaded the night before. She returned to the boys' room where she sat down by the window, nudged the window up two inches and pushed the draperies back just enough to see through to the shadow flecked lawn beyond. She propped the shotgun on the windowsill and waited. She could not hear her men or Code. Tensed and with her finger on the trigger, she waited. A figure emerged from the woods, followed by two more. As she watched, they split off, two heading towards the back of the house. One sprinted towards where she lay in wait. She heard Code's frenzied barking, followed by two quick gunshots and then silence. The remaining man was in her line of sight. She didn't hesitate. The man dropped just as Quint and Gerald came running around the side of the house. They skidded to an amazed stop. Both looked toward the window with mouths agape. She reckoned she had just shown them a thing or two.

She heard Quint swear. "What in the hell. Man, you've got yourself some woman there."

"You're telling me! Let's get these fuckers onto the back porch and turn the light on. If they're not dead, we'll see what we can learn. If they are, we need to put them in the boat and dump them in the Chesapeake." Gerald left Quint standing guard and walked over to the bedroom window. "In case, I didn't tell you, Miss Annie Oakley, I love you, woman!"

"I know." Jill laughed, "Now, clean up the mess while I check on our boys."

She paused, a worried frown knit her brow, "Honey, do you think anymore are out there?"

"I doubt it, but it wouldn't hurt to keep an eye out. Are you up to it?"

"No problem. Just be careful."

"Hey, I've got you watching my back."

"Be careful anyway," she ordered.

Code curled up on the ground below her window as the men picked up the man she had shot and hauled his body around back. They repeated the procedure with the other two. All three were dead. They searched the bodies and found no identification. All three looked Arabic. Without a word, Quint grabbed the legs of one while Gerald picked up the shoulders and they carried the first body to the boat. They repeated the procedure with the other two. Untying the mooring line, Quint jumped in the boat. The minute his feet hit the deck, Gerald gunned the engine and they headed out into the bay where they heaved the bodies overboard.

They sat there for a minute under a starlit sky. Finally Gerald broke the silence. "I don't know who you are Quint, but you damned sure aren't some wimpy nerd like we all thought. You've got smarts out the kazoo, but somewhere along the way you picked up skills to rival my SEAL buddies. Who in the hell trained you?"

Quint laughed, "I trained myself, hotshot."

"No damn way."

"Really. I went online, did some research and taught myself. It's amazing what you can learn if you try."

"Holy shit. The government spends millions doing what you did for nothing." Gerald roared with laughter. "You are the best joke on us all I have ever seen. Dammit man, we're going to have to figure out something else to do with you. I think I need to introduce you to my friend Buster Walton. Something tells me he is going to purely love your ass. He's looking to hire, too."

"My stock is sure rising. That's the second job offer I've had in the last couple of days."

"Yeah...me and who else?"

"Your buddy across the pond."

"Bastard."

"It's alright. I turned him down. But, it doesn't hurt to keep one's options open."

When they returned to the house, Jill was in the kitchen with a Royal Flush mixed and waiting for the three of them.

"I thought we could use something to settle our nerves," she said as she handed a shot glass to each of the men.

Quint had never had the drink before so he watched Gerald and Jill toss theirs' back, before following suit. "Wow. I could get used to this stuff."

"It's our favorite," Gerald remarked as he watched Jill pour another round. "Let's down this and see if we can get some sleep. Mine's been cut short two nights in a row now. Come morning, we probably need to think about a safe house for a while."

"Y'all go on to bed. I'll get the boys from the tub and tuck them back in for you."

"Thank you, Quint. You're going to make a good father." Jill asked, "Did you grow up with younger brothers and sisters?"

"Unfortunately, no. My parents were in their forties when I came along. My mother said she had found all she wanted in me and was afraid to try again. My dad said that after me, he was for sure afraid to try again. I don't think they ever figured out which one was right."

Gerald laughed and patted him on the back. "I think we are all a mixed bag anyway, so don't even try to figure it out."

With the boys tucked back into their beds, Quint signaled for Code to follow him to the guestroom. Code turned his back on him and lay down between the two twin beds. He thumbed his tail a couple of times and put his head down on his front paws. Quint whispered, "Traitor."

The sun was well up when he rolled over in bed to find three pairs of eyes staring at him. Georgie, Jimbo and Code stood beside the bed. Georgie and Jimbo giggled and Code gave a soft bark, before all three climbed onto the bed with him.

Georgie, the older one, said, "Please, Uncle Quint, don't take Code away. We really love him."

Before falling asleep, an idea had come to him that he wanted to run by Gerald before saying anything to the boys. "Aw, come on Georgie. You know I can't give my buddy away. Would you give Jimbo here away if someone asked you?"

"Oh, I know. You take Jimbo and I'll take Code." George looked at him with eyes as big saucers.

Quint watched tears gather in Jimbo's eyes. "Hey, Jimbo, he's only kidding you. Besides, you are a neat kid and I wouldn't mind having you a bit, but your family loves you so much they couldn't do without you. I love Code a little bit like that. He's about all the family I have left now."

George studied him a moment with a sad expression on his

face, "Are you an orphan, Quint?"

"I guess I never thought of it in quite that way since I am all grown up, but yes, I guess I am."

Jimbo piped up, "That's okay, Uncle Quint. We will adopt you to be our brother. That way we get you *and* Code."

Quint watched both boys nodding vigorously and laughed. "I think your mom and dad might object to having a big old guy like me for a son. Why don't I just stay your adopted uncle? Now you boys scoot. I need to get up and talk to your parents about something."

After the boys left the room with a joyful Code chasing at their heels, Quint pulled on a T-shirt and jeans, slipped his feet into a pair of loafers and strolled out to the kitchen where he found the boys at the counter with bowls of cereal in front of them. Their parents were laughing as the two dug into the cereal with relish.

Jill looked over at him and grinned. "You would think we've been starving them."

Quint smiled in return. "After breakfast, I have an idea I want to run by the two of you."

"I was going to start packing. I don't know where we are going yet until I talk to Thomas, but we can't stay here any longer." Gerald's face was grim as he looked at his wife.

"I know, that's what I want to talk to you about."

"Why don't we hold off on our breakfast while you tell us what you have in mind." Gerald nodded toward the deck overlooking the brilliant blue water of the Chesapeake. "It's gorgeous out. Let's step outside for a minute or two while the boys work on their cereal."

Quint followed the couple onto the deck. They turned to

face him with their backs to the cypress railing that ran around the deck and waited expectantly.

"Gerald, you know about my place at Figure Eight. What you don't know is that it is not just a simple beach house. I have a secure bunker and all kinds of other security devices there that can keep us all safe. As you already know, the island has a gatehouse that allows only authorized vehicles to come on the island. If the Hendersons had been willing to use the main house, they might have been able to reach safety before the killer got to them. Even the grounds there are monitored by pressure sensors. All they had to do was turn on the security system. They always laughed my concerns off as paranoia. Now I am so sorry I didn't insist. I thought I had covered my tracks and no one could trace the property back to me, but I should have known better. At any rate, it is a lovely site with the beach for the boys to play on. With Code and us to protect them, they should be safe. It would help if the Wilmington office could send an asset team to patrol the area on shifts. Since these bastards already tried a strike there and failed, they are not likely to go back...particularly if we can create a plausible subterfuge."

"From what I could see the other night, it's gorgeous. I know the kids and Jill would like it far better than the safe house in Stanton." Gerald looked at his wife, "Honey, the place is a mansion. You are going to absolutely love it. I think you will enjoy painting there, too. We can have our guys pack up your painting things and I'll have Buster Walton pick them up and bring them to us. We can trust him."

Gerald turned to Quint, "Do you have room for Buster and his crew?"

"Sure. They can have the Hendersons' cottage."

"I think I would prefer to use them for the moment rather than Agency men." Gerald raised his eyebrows at his wife, "Will you trust us on this, Baby Cakes?"

"You know I do and don't forget, I know how to fight bad guys, too." Jill added, "Now that's settled, come on in and I'll make us some breakfast."

After they had all eaten, Jill sent the boys to their room to collect their things with Gerald to supervise while she packed her own clothes and the few things Gerald had brought. "Honey!' she called out, "When you talk to Buster, have him pack up some clothes for you. You have practically nothing here."

"Will do."

Quint's own things were packed and by the front door, when the couple emerged with bags and kids in tow. The three adults carried things to the car while the boys collected Code's toys to take along. Code took it all in before lying down on the porch with one eye closed and the other watching the scurrying about. When everything was loaded and the kids strapped into their seats, Code ambled down to the cars and stood watching to see where he should go. Gerald motioned for Quint to drive the car they had used the night before along with his luggage and dog. He would drive his wife's car with his family. Cautioning Quint to stay within sight at all times, they drove from the driveway onto the road off the island. On the way out, Jill used her phone to call Chester Norris and tell him they were leaving. Chester sounded sad when he commented that their stay had been short enough to preclude any visiting. After promising another visit soon, Jill rang off.

"I think Chester is really lonely. It's too bad this mess cropped up and we had no time to spend with him. He's been wonderful about watching out for the place."

"When all of this is behind us, we'll come back. I'm due some time off."

"I hear you. I don't mean to gripe, but every time you think you can take a vacation, something comes up to interfere."

Gerald glanced over at his wife before reaching for her hand, "I know, honey. Let's just be positive about this one. You are going to love Figure Eight. I suspected Quint came from some serious money, but after seeing the house there, I know it. It is spectacular and the view is beautiful. You can see the ocean on one side and the sound on the other. I was there at night and under unfortunate conditions, but I saw enough to realize just how special it is. We'll just consider this a vacation of sorts. Quint and I both need to stay out of the limelight just now, so we will be with you. I'll bet you'll be disgusted to see me morning, noon, and night."

"I wouldn't count on that. Besides, we have built in entertainment and a babysitter: Code and Quint. I can thing of a thing or two we can do with all this time on our hands."

"So can I." Gerald paused, "Unfortunately, we also have to work. Quint assures me he has a hell of a computer system and it's secure. If it is, it's not all going to be playtime. Not only that, but we have to be careful until we can take out whoever is after us."

"I don't want to deal with the negative just now," her voice cracked. Jill looked out the window. She had killed a man the night before and she wanted to forget it. She had never done that before. Regardless of the fact she was protecting the ones she loved, it was still an ugly thing and she was not handling it as well as she wanted.

Gerald sensed her mood and the reason for it, "Don't think about it, Jill. We all did what we had to do. Otherwise, it might have been us that died, and our boys. I realize that doesn't make it easy or pretty. But sometimes life isn't. It particularly isn't in my line of work. I just hate the hell out of it when it affects my family. It makes me feel like I let you down. I thought when I quit fieldwork and took a desk job all of this would be behind me. I was stupid to believe that. None of us are safe anymore. 9-11 taught us that if nothing else."

Chapter 11

"To hell with that, you whore." Forsyth was beyond furious. London was a disaster. The hits he had ordered had all failed, and now the bitch wanted to quit on him.

"I mean it. I can't do this anymore. Mr. Thomas made an appointment for me at 1:00 tomorrow. The memo with the information about Quint Cord that Mr. Williams left on his desk is gone. I didn't move it and Mr. Williams has not been in the office since. On top of that, I found what looks like finger print powder on his desk and mine. I think they suspect me. I'm going to resign today. Please, don't ask me to do anything else for you." Marlowe's voice caught, "I'm telling my husband tonight that I am quitting and why. If he doesn't love me enough, I'll have to accept it and deal with the consequences. I just want you to leave me alone."

Forsyth force himself to project calmness. "I got you into this mess, and I'll get you out. Don't make any hasty decisions today. At 10:00 tomorrow morning, make an excuse to leave your office and go to the parking area. I'll have a car waiting with my attorney in it. He will advise you how to handle this. After he does some research, he will return at 1:00 and attend the meeting with you."

"I'm not sure about that. Won't I look guilty if I show up with an attorney?"

"It's just a precaution. Meet my attorney as I said. You can discuss it with him."

"I suppose that's okay. How will I know which car?"

"You won't need to know. He will recognize you. Do you have a red dress or red scarf that is suitable for the office?"

"Yes, but I don't wear bright colors to work."

"Forsyth bit his tongue to keep from snapping at the bitch, "Then wear a red scarf with your business clothes. I'm sure it will be okay to wear a red scarf. Now, remember: be in the parking lot at 10:00. He'll pick you up and drive around for a few minutes while you talk."

Marlowe agreed and hung up. She felt as though her perfect life was collapsing around her. She had not yet told her husband that she was three months pregnant with their first child. Now, she couldn't. First she would have to see if he could accept her and still love her despite her past. If he could not, she would go back to Little Rock and move in with her aunt until she could get on her feet and support her baby. As a well-paid surgical specialist, her husband had insisted she keep the money she earned from working, as they had no need for it. She had almost $52,000 in her savings account. That would support her while she couldn't work and help her rent a place to live after the baby came. Facing her husband was the hardest thing she had ever had to do in her life. Tomorrow after her meeting, she would tell Robbie and ask for his forgiveness for deceiving him about her past. After that Douglas Forsyth would have no more hold on her.

*****

Robbie knew his wife too well not to recognize when she was upset about something. Although she had welcomed him home with the usual kiss and hug, she seemed down to him. He waited for her to tell him what the problem might be, but she did not bring it up. After a somewhat silent dinner, he reached for her hand as she began to rise from the table, "Honey, what's bothering you?"

Refusing to meet his eyes for he would sense how troubled she was, she replied, "It was just a long day at work, but I'll be fine. Don't worry, okay?'

"You know if the job becomes a problem you can quit. You don't need to work. I'm sure you could find something to do so you aren't bored, volunteer at the hospital, whatever."

"I've been thinking about quitting. In fact, I plan to tell the Agency tomorrow that I'm resigning my job."

"You must have had a worse day than you're letting on." He stroked her hand before gently asking, "Want to tell me about it, Marlowe?"

"Could we talk about it tomorrow night? I really don't want to get into it tonight."

"Sure, if that's better for you. But, don't blame me for worrying. I don't want my beautiful loving wife to ever be upset about anything."

"I know. I love you so very much. Just bear with me."

"That goes without saying. Why don't you sit here and finish your wine while I get the dishes. You've barely touched it."

"No, I'll help. I guess I'm really not in the mood for wine."

"Alright, leave the wine, and go get a nice relaxing bath. I'll come up as soon as I finish here and give you a nice massage. Will that work?"

She ducked her head so he could not see the tears that threatened to spill from her eyes, "You spoil me, honey."

"I intend to every day for the rest of our lives." He pulled her up from the table, kissed her lips, and gave a pat to her fanny, "Up you go."

They curled up in bed later and he was soon asleep, but Marlowe couldn't stand the thought that this might be their last night together after she confessed the truth. She wanted to relish every moment of him holding her. The moonlight coming through the window cast his features in silhouette. She drank the sight in, trying to impress it on her memory in case it had to last forever. Morning found her with circles under her eyes and a raging case of morning sickness. She barely made it to the bathroom before she vomited into the toilet. Heaving repeatedly, she at last sank to the floor and wiped her mouth with toilet paper. She flinched when the door opened.

"Are you okay, babe?"

She nodded her head weakly, "I think I've caught some kind of bug."

Robbie laughed, "Have you forgotten I'm a doctor? So, when were you planning to tell me I'm going to be a father?"

Marlowe lifted her head in surprise, "Oh, no. It's not that."

"All the signs are there, sweetheart. Let me make you an appointment with a good Ob-Gyn. There are several that work in our office suite."

She started shaking her head negatively, but he interrupted. "We need to make sure, so don't say no. I'll see if I can get an appointment for tomorrow. I'll call you later and let you know. Now, can I help you up? Do you want me to call into work for you and say you're not feeling well?"

"I'll be fine, really. I need to go into work today. There are several things I have to take care of."

"I'll get you some toast and coffee and we'll see."

Marlowe forced herself to rise and shower while he was

gone. When he returned with the coffee, she ignored it and concentrated on getting a few bites of the dry toast down. Feeling better, she smiled, "Thanks. That's just what the doctor, ordered so to speak. I already feel better."

"Good. So, do you go, or stay here and curl up with a good book?"

She forced a smile and made her voice light when she replied, "Maybe tomorrow."

Marlowe was nearly out the door when she remembered the red scarf. Dashing back to the bedroom she grabbed it from the drawer and hurried out to her car. Robbie had already left for his office, but before leaving he had picked a rose from the garden and tucked it under the windshield wiper. Marlowe saw it and beamed. Surely everything would be fine. They loved one another so much it had to work out. When she reached her office, she tucked her purse and the scarf in the right hand drawer of her desk, and checked and answered emails. While she waited for the clock to crawl its way around to ten, she decided she would write her story and let her husband read it. Somehow it felt easier to write it than to tell it. At five minutes before the hour, she saved the unfinished letter. She then grabbed her red scarf from the drawer. Seeing no need for her purse, she left it in the drawer.

She tied the scarf around her neck as she left the building and walked into the parking lot. A black sedan that had been waiting at the curb pulled up and the passenger side door opened. She hesitated by the open door. The driver was casually dressed, not what she was expecting a lawyer to look like. "Who are you?"

"Forsythe sent me. I'm your new attorney. Get in, Mrs.

Hollins. I don't have time to waste."

Something about him set alarm bells ringing. "I told the Congressman I don't need an attorney."

The rear door swung open. A large Middle Eastern looking man jumped out and shoved her into the front passenger seat. Before she could open the door and escape, she felt cold steel pressed into her neck. Marlowe screamed, "Let me out!"

"Shut your damned trap. You make another sound of any kind and I'll blow your fucking head off."

In that moment, she knew her life was finished. These men would never allow her to get away. Holding her hands over her belly, she closed her eyes and prayed. The memory of Robbie's face in the moonlight came back to her and tears seeped beneath her lashes as she choked back sobs. Twenty minutes later the car stopped. Marlowe opened her eyes to see that they were on a dirt path surrounded by woods. With panic-stricken eyes she turned to the driver, "Please don't do this. I'm going to have a baby. Let me talk to Mr. Forsyth. I'm sure this is all just a bad mistake."

"Shut the fuck up and get out of the car."

The big guy in back got out and pulled her door open when she refused to leave the car. Reaching in, he snatched her out hurting her arm. She squealed in pain as she struggled to gain her balance. He ignored her screams as he pushed her ahead of him into the edge of the woods. The last thing she heard was the singing of birds in the branches overhead. It seemed like such a peaceful place. And then all went black.

Jamal Hussein picked up his phone and called the boss, "Your little problem is taken care of."

"Make it look like she was raped before she was shot."

"Pretty as she is that shouldn't be a problem, even if I've never done it to a corpse before. Next time how about letting me know before we shoot. I think I might enjoy it more."

"You're not getting paid to have fun. Just do it. Rough her up a little so it looks like she fought you. Both you and Mohammed put your peckers in her. I don't want the cops suspecting any other reason for her death."

*****

When Robbie arrived home that night, his wife's car was not in the driveway. Thinking she might have worked late, he opened a beer and settled in the family room to watch the evening news. When that was done, he picked up his cell phone and called Marlowe's office number. When she did not pick up, he tried her cell and again no answer. It was unlike her not to let him know when she was going to be late and more unlike her not to answer her cell when he called. He walked into the kitchen and grabbed another beer from the fridge. Walking outside he paced the deck as he watched the stars appear. Every five minutes he called her cell phone. At eleven that night, he was past alarmed. Looking on her desk, he found the phone number for Jill Williams and dialed the home phone. Again, there was no answer so he tried the cell. Jill answered on the second ring.

"Mrs. Williams, I am Robbie Hollins. I know Marlowe is a friend of yours and works for your husband. I am very concerned that she is not home yet and I cannot reach her either on the office phone or her cell phone. Do you know if something is going on at the Agency that might preclude her calling?"

"I'm sorry Dr. Hollins, but I have no idea. Let me put my

husband on the phone."

Gerald took the phone his wife handed him and asked, "What can I do for you Dr. Hollins?"

Again Robbie repeated what he had told Jill.

Gerald listened intently, puzzled himself by the woman's disappearance and wondering if it was linked to the leak in the office. If it was the man had reason to worry about his wife. "I'll call security and have them check her office. Give me her license number and a description of her car and I'll have them check the parking lot and see if it's there. I'll get back to you the minute I hear something. Is this number good?"

"Yes. I'll be here."

Gerald waited anxiously while the security detail checked his secretary's office and then the parking lot. Fred Massey called back to say that she was not in the building and her car was still in the lot. Thinking hard, Gerald said, "Check her desk. See if there is a note or anything that might explain where she is. Call me back as soon as you've done it. Her husband is understandably anxious."

Five minutes later, Gerald's phone rang again, "Sir, there's no note but her purse with her cell phone and keys are in the desk drawer. Wherever she is, it doesn't look like she planned on leaving."

"Start checking. Get someone to open her computer and check anything she might have in it. I'll have Dr. Hollins email his wife's photo to you. Go through the security camera footage for today and see what you find. We've got enough coverage in the building and parking lot to find a gnat."

"Will do. I'll call you as soon as we find something."

Gerald shook his head at his wife's inquiring look, "It

doesn't look good honey."

He called Hollins and gave him as much as he knew. Robbie promised to email a photo immediately to the number Gerald gave him.

"We have cameras everywhere. We'll find her. Try not to worry for now."

"That's a lot easier said than done. We suspect she's pregnant and she wasn't feeling well this morning. She was planning on quitting, but there was something she said she had to do first. I do hope you find her soon. I'm about to go nuts just sitting here."

"Man, I can sympathize. Trust us. We'll find her."

Gerald drove south on Interstate 95 with his mind only half on the traffic. He could not avoid the conclusion that the fake file he left on his desk had led to a bad end for the woman. When they reached the North Carolina line, Jill had had enough. He was so distracted he had once again nearly hit a car before breaking at the last moment to avoid a collision. "Honey, let me drive. We all need a bathroom break and something to eat. Let's stop at the next place and I'll drive the rest of the way. Just call Quint and tell him to pick a spot and we'll follow."

Gerald's phone rang just as they turned on Interstate 40 and headed east towards Wilmington. "Yeah, what do you have?"

"There was the beginning of what looks like a confession letter on her computer. It wasn't finished. I'll send it to you. And that is only half of the bad news. We have camera footage of her in the parking lot. This car comes cruising up, she opens the passenger door and talks a few minutes and then it looks like she's going to leave when the rear door opens and this big guy gets out and shoves her in."

"Damn. See if you can get a facial recognition on the guy."

"Judging from the angle, I doubt it. But, we'll try. I sure would hate to be her husband right now, boss. This looks bad."

"That it does."

Gerald hung up and waited a couple of minutes wondering what to say to Marlowe's husband before reluctantly making the call.

Chapter 12

Gerald swore softly under his breath at the realization that his secretary was being blackmailed and why. Even worse, than her confession was the fact she had reached the point in the letter when she appeared to be ready to reveal the blackmailer when the letter was left unfinished. There was no way he could run a database to discover everyone in Washington that was in Little Rock when she was a working girl. The possibilities were staggering. They sat on the porch at Quint's house on Figure Eight staring at the breakers rolling onto the beach. Quint occupied the chair next to him. Both men were sipping on a glass of wine. Jill was reading the exhausted kids a bedtime story.

"I guess from that sigh you're a little frustrated by something."

"I am angry as hell with myself that I didn't do a better job having my secretary vetted before hiring her. I've pretty much got to get over that ass kicking and figure out who wanted her dead. It's a fucking shame she stopped on the confessional letter just before revealing the bastard's name."

"You figure she's dead then?"

"Read this and tell me what you think?" Gerald handed his cell phone to Quint and waited while he read the unfinished letter.

Quint whistled. "Yeah, she's been offed. You say there's a security video showing her being pushed into a car, so why not have her husband look at it and see if he notices anything."

"Damn. The man is crazy with worry as it is. I'm not sure I can lay this on him. But, then again, if it's a chance to find some clue as to what happened to his wife I have no other choice."

Gerald made the call. Quint waited until he was finished.

"So, what's the game plan?"

"Security is on the way to pick him up. We're bringing him in. We'll show him the video and then we're going to tuck him away somewhere until we are sure he's not a mark. If this bastard thinks she might have told him something, his life is in danger, too."

"You think she kept it from him based on the letter, and frankly so do I. But you're right. Whoever is behind this doesn't know that. Are you going to let him read the letter she started writing to him?"

Gerald shook his head, "I considered it but it would only hurt more. If I were Hollins, I wouldn't want to know. Let him grieve the woman he knew and not the one she was before."

"I agree."

*****

At the Agency monitoring room Hollins watched the security reel, a sob catching in his throat when he saw his wife being shoved into the waiting car. Something didn't seem right about her to him. Looking at the agent who had introduced himself as Charles Burke, he said, "Mr. Burke, would you run this again, please?"

Again he watched, and then a third time before it hit him. "She never wore scarves, and unless I'm mistaken, that is a red scarf she particularly hated. It's hard to tell from the distance, but I'm pretty sure that is the one. She said someone she hated gave it to her. I asked her why she kept it if she hated the scarf and who it was from, but she just said she kept it as a reminder."

"Do you know 'what reminder' she was referring to?"

"No, she never would say. She just said it was long ago and no longer important. I'm surprised she wore a scarf, much less that one."

When his assistant, Jerry McCree, came to take Hollins to the safe house, Burke immediately called Gerald Williams. "I have something. You will have to decide how to use it. Seems to me there was some kind of sign that would make her recognizable to someone that didn't know her."

He proceeded to repeat everything that Hollins had said about the scarf.

When Burke was finished, Gerald remarked, "I agree. It was a signal. That means this meeting was set up in advance, maybe the day before. Get on the phone log and get me the names and numbers of everyone she called the day before or who called her. If you don't find anything to flag there, go back for the last week. Also pull her email log and see if anything is on it. You have her cell phone, so do the same search on it."

"On it." Burke hung up without saying goodbye. It was a habit of his.

Gerald took a sip of his wine and settled back in his chair. Glancing over at Quint, he asked, "How did you ever get in the code breaking business?"

"It was always a hobby of mine. My dad wanted me to go into business with him but I just wasn't interested. I went to the University of North Carolina and studied business my first year trying to keep him happy. I finally said to hell with it and switched to history. That's when I discovered some of the famous codes used throughout history and I was hooked. A Masters degree in history didn't do much to qualify me for a wide array of jobs, so after several months of nothing I went to a job fair. I was just wondering around, not much interested in anything, when this guy walked up and started a conversation. He never did come right out and say for whom he worked, just said there was something about me he thought might suit the profile of what he was looking for. He asked he what I had majored in and what I liked to do. When I said breaking codes, his eyes lit up and I knew I had found a job. I found out later that he works for the CIA and while he was looking to fill a different category, he realized he could use me, too."

"Well, that explains the first part. So, tell me why you developed the other skills we knew nothing about?"

"You mean the physical training, I assume?"

"Yeah. What caused you to go for that?"

"It's really motivating when you realize you're swimming in a tank full of sharks. My first job was an eye opener. Some bad guys wanted my ass badly...badly enough to try to kill me. I don't know how I did it, but I got away through sheer dumb luck. I swore then and there I was going to be as bad an ass as anyone they could throw at me."

"Don't tell me you risk your life just because you like solving the codes we toss at you?"

"Hell no! I'm doing it because I love this country and I don't like what's happening to it. If we don't get a handle on these radical Islamic terrorists, they're going to destroy western civilization as we know it. Maybe mine is a small contribution, but I'm damn well going to do everything I can to get them. This politically correct bullshit is just going to get us dead."

"I agree. Sometimes I think the media and the politicians are as big a threat as ISIS." Gerald nodded back towards the house, "How in the hell did you figure out the security you have here? It's like a damn bunker!"

"That was fun. Again, I got on the computer and went looking. Watched some thriller movies, and then just sat around thinking on it and things kind of evolved from there. I did some neat stuff in my Raleigh house, too. That's probably what saved me when that shooter came for me while I was running in the park. I'd rigged the garage with tunnel access and a back wall that would lift up dumping me out on a back alley rather than the street."

"Amazing."

Jill walked out with the wine bottle and a glass for herself. She poured them both a refill before joining them. "What's amazing?"

"The talents our boy here has that I knew nothing about."

"And you a real spy...imagine that." Jill laughed and winked at her husband.

"Yeah, well, I'm rusty since I got out of field work."

Quint smiled at Jill, "Did you get those two live-wires settled down?"

"Once I agreed to let Code sleep with them. I hope you don't mind?"

"Nah. Code owns the house and me to. It's pretty much his say around here, so don't worry about it."

"Thank you for suggesting we come, Quint. I adore the house and can barely wait to see the view in daylight. The boys are excited, too, and eager to get on the beach in the morning and do some exploring. Do you think that will be okay?"

"Gerald, do you know when your team is arriving?" Quint asked.

"They should be here first thing in the morning. Jill, I think you should keep the kids in the house until Buster and his men get here, check things out, and set up a perimeter watch. We can also check angles and see where in the yard is safe from snipers, even though I think that is unlikely since these houses aren't like rental property. There's nothing we can do about the beach, but with the island being private it's going to be a lot harder for them to mount any kind of daylight attack...except maybe from the sea. We'll post someone around the clock in the Widow's walk, too. Hopefully they aren't onto our location yet, but I'd rather be safe than sorry."

It was late when they left the porch and went to their bedrooms. Quint lay in his bed, his hand draped off the side searching for his dog when he realized Code had defected in favor of sleeping with the boys. Quint chuckled under his breath, so much for loyalty. However, he damn well would buy them at least one dog. No way were they getting his buddy.

*****

Dr. Hollins got the news he had been dreading two days later. One of the agents assigned to protect him came into the kitchen while he was sitting at the table reading the Washington Post. Robbie could tell by the expression on the man's face it wasn't going to be good.

"Tell me."

"I'm sorry man. Some kids were playing in the woods and came across a body that matches the description of your wife. I hate like hell to ask this, but we need you to come in and do a positive ID for us." The agent waited while Robbie choked back sobs as he tried to gain some kind of composure.

His voice was dull when he responded, "Sure. Can you tell how she died?"

"It looks like it was a gun shot wound. We'll know more after the autopsy." The agent was not going to tell this man his wife had been raped and her breasts mutilated. Some things family just didn't need to deal with in his opinion. If someone else wanted to dump that on the man they could do, it but he would not.

Robbie was a doctor. He had seen corpses before, but he was not prepared for seeing the face of the woman he loved on one. He stood woodenly as the coroner in the morgue peeled the sheet back to expose the face. Despite the bruises, he recognized Marlowe instantly. At the same moment his knees gave way and he grabbed the edge of the gurney to support himself pulling the sheet further down on her body revealing the tops of her breasts. Wheeling back, he turned and heaved his breakfast all over the floor before he could reach a basin.

"Oh, Christ. I"m sorry," he stammered as he wiped his face with the wet towel and assistant handed him. "What kind of sick animal would do this to her?"

"If it is any comfort to you, she was dead when that happened. There wasn't enough blood for her to have been alive. I think they wanted it to look like a rape. I'm not so sure. I have a hunch it was the gunshot in the back of the head that killed her before any of the rest happened. If that's the case she did not suffer the torture this would have inflicted had she been alive. I'm sorry, Dr. Hollins. No man should have to look at the woman he loves in this condition. Hopefully we'll find the perpetrators."

Robbie shook his head. "I hope the police find them before I do. I can't promise I won't take justice into my own hands."

"I believe the Feds are on this one since I gather she was an employee of the CIA. I suspect they are looking to see if there was any kind of tie-in to her job. Nobody is better than the guys that will be working this case."

Jerry McCree, the agent that had first broken the news to him, took Robbie by the elbow. "I hate to do it, Doc, but we need you at the Agency to answer some questions and look at that security tape again to see if you recognize the man that snatched her."

Like someone in a trance, Robbie followed Jerry out to the waiting black SUV. He looked up and asked, "Don't you guys have any other kind of vehicle?"

"Nope. This is pretty much it. This one is a lot more than it looks. It's built like a tank. We're going to take good care of you until we figure out whether or not they're after you."

"I need to call my office. Chris Wafford, my partner, is going to have a cow when I tell him he's going to be covering for me for the foreseeable future."

Jerry assured him, "No problem, but you'll need to call from our office. Your phone is off limits until we get this sorted. You did remove the cell phone battery as I asked, didn't you?"

"Yeah. That's been done."

Jerry kept up a steady chatter keeping Hollins distracted. That was fine with Robbie Hollins as he did not want to be so overcome with emotion that he would be unable to help with questions the Agency might want to ask. He was content to lose himself in idle conversation. He was hanging on by a thread and doing his best to avoid facing what was happening to his life. Sooner or later, he knew he would need some private time to let his emotions out.

In the Langley screening room, Robbie once again watched Marlowe walk out to the car, talk to the driver, begin to back away, when the thug in back sprang out and pushed her in. He felt utter hatred consume him as he studied the bastard. He had never seen him before, but if he ever did, he was a dead man. To hell with the cops! His medical training had taught him enough ways to kill someone, he could do it and they would never know. All he had to do was get close. There was a profile view of the driver, but even with enhancement it was too vague to give any clue to identity.

Chapter 13

Forsyth sat in his red leather swivel chair mulling what had gone wrong. The meeting at the Willard had been abruptly cancelled leaving his Washington plan in shambles. Now he would need to devise a new one to eliminate both the President and Vice President while keeping the focus on what would look like a terrorist plot from outside the country. It would take some planning, but he had done it before and could do it again. The nagging question was whether or not the failure in both England and Washington was the result of someone catching on to what he was up to, or if it were mere coincidence. He was not one to accept coincidence without proof. He had not yet confirmed the Paris event. The more he thought about it the more he thought about doing a diversionary tactic in Paris prior to his real goal to see if it would be interrupted. Were that to happen, he would know he had either been hacked or his code was broken.

He looked up from his computer when his wife entered the room. She had begun to annoy him. He did not like being annoyed and if it continued, he would have to see to changing the situation. He still hesitated at that. He liked her docile attitude both in bed and out. Her type was increasingly hard to find. Most women as beautiful as she had more ego. He liked her being afraid of him and pleading with him not to beat her. He felt like more of a man when he had forcibly taken her after leaving her bloodied from his fists. Just thinking about it made him hard.

"Come here," he commanded, pleased when fear flared in her eyes.

Rena warned herself to keep her voice steady and calm. "I just wanted to see if you were ready for dinner. The cook says we need to come at once or her soufflé will be ruined."

"I said come here! To hell with the damned cook."

Rena walked forward with eyes downcast so he could not see the hatred she felt for him. When she stood in front of him, he reached up and pushed her to her knees.

"Undo me," his eyes directed her to a rampant erection.

With her reluctance apparent, despite her desire to hide it from him, she did not comply quickly enough. That was all the excuse Douglas needed to viciously slam his fist into her left breast. Gasping in pain, she hurriedly undid his trousers. She blinked tears from her eyes as she bent forward and took him in her mouth. He shoved her head down until she was gagging. Struggling to keep from throwing up, she began the manipulations that she knew he enjoyed. After it was finished, he snatched her head up by the hair and snarled, "Tell the damned cook to make me something else. I need to finish what I was working on when you strutted your ass in here. Now get out and leave me alone. I'll eat dinner when I'm damned ready. I'm the boss in this house, not the fucking cook."

Rena slowly rose. She didn't look at him but at the computer screen where she read the partially finished email. With a photographic memory he was totally unaware of, she was storing everything she saw. Gradually a picture was coming into focus that told her the kind of man he was. He was far from the man he presented to the public and the one he had pretended to be when he courted her. When she had enough, she would make him pay for the years of humiliation and pain he had brought her. But, she had to be careful. There was no doubt in her mind that he would kill her if he suspected what she was up to. The minute she left the office she hurried to find a paper and pen. Jotting down the numbers she had seen on the screen, she tucked the note into her bra wondering what it meant. She then went to the kitchen to tell the cook that her husband wanted dinner later.

Rena sat on the stool in the kitchen across from Teresa who had been her first hire for the household. Teresa was a gifted cook and totally self-taught. Through the years they had become friends. Although she had never said it outright anymore than Rena herself, she knew that the woman hated Douglas Forsyth as much as she did. Teresa was not so ignorant of the abuse his wife suffered. Unexplained bruises and tear-filled eyes did much to inform. Unconscious of her actions, Rena rubbed her breast that was still throbbing with pain. Through the silk of her blouse she could feel the lump rising where he had punched her.

"Are you hurting, Miss Rena?" Teresa knew the question was an invasion of a privacy she had respected, but she could no longer hold back.

"Oh, it's nothing, really."

"Humph...I suspect I know what kind of nothing you're talking about. I don't know why you put up with this mess. You need to fix yourself up and get out of here. You don't have to live this way. You are so putdown and meek that you are afraid to even be yourself. Here you are dressing all dowdy-like and trying to blend into the background all the time. You are a beautiful woman and a smart one. Stop hiding it. There has got to be something better for you than that devil."

Rena watched as slow tears filled the seams on Teresa's mahogany colored face. "Shh, I'm going to be fine. I just wish it were easier. God only knows I do. I just don't know how to get away from him. You don't know him, Teresa. He's capable of some bad things...really bad. You need to be careful, too. Never let him suspect how you feel."

Teresa shook her head. Her voice was bitter when she said, "No you're not going to be fine. Not if you keep staying here. Sooner or later he's going to hurt you bad. You think I don't know how you ended up with that broken arm last year?"

Rena whispered, "I have a plan. I just need a little more time. Now we better change the subject. I don't want him to know that I confide in you. He would fire you in a heartbeat if he suspected we even talked about more than the menu."

"Lord, I know that's the truth."

Forsyth hesitated just outside the kitchen door. He had heard enough to be royally ticked off, but he squelched it for the moment. He would deal with his wife later. If the cook were not superior, he would have fired her on the spot. As it was, he liked having the cook make meals his guests raved over better than having his wife. Clearing his throat he entered the kitchen.

Both women looked up in fear. They dared not meet one another's eyes. "Darling, we were not expecting you so soon."

"I know. I didn't want to keep that soufflé waiting. I remember from experience just how delicious it is," he smiled at Teresa as he said it. "I don't know how my wife got so lucky when she hired you, but I'm glad she did."

"Thank you, sir," Teresa said as she stood. "I'll have your dinner on the dining room table in just a few minutes."

Douglas turned to his wife, "Shall we go in?"

"Yes, of course. Perhaps we can enjoy a little wine while Teresa is getting our dinner ready."

As Teresa served the meal, Rena sipped her wine and avoided looking at her husband. The dinner was delicious, but to her it was difficult to appreciate, as she never knew what might await her afterwards. She leaned over and poured more wine into her husband's empty glass. He had already emptied most of the first bottle and was well into the second. She sipped slowly for it would never do for him to think she was deliberately getting him intoxicated by not drinking herself. She hoped he would get so stumbling drunk, he would pass out on his office sofa leaving her in peace.

She watched Douglas studying her over the rim of his glass as he inhaled the aroma of his wine. Not knowing what he was thinking, Rena forced herself to remain calm and to talk about inconsequential things. It would never do to let him know how unnerved she was by the scrutiny. She wondered if he knew she had copied the coded messages on his computer. Since they were in a code she did not understand, she doubted that was the issue. The fact that she and Teresa had been talking when he entered the kitchen was more problematic. He would be royally angry if he had heard all of the conversation. If he had, her life was not worth living. She was not stupid as he assumed...far from it. But, as for the day she allowed him into her life, she had to question her sanity. Somehow she would have to protect what little information she had and assure that if something were to happen to her it would get to the right people. Through her husband she had met many government officials and their wives. Surely one of them could take what she knew and what she suspected to the right people. The question was who? The bigger question and the one that caused the greatest fear was whether or not she would have the time and opportunity to do it? She was as sequestered as any wife under Sharia law...and she had long suspected why. The people she could contact in person were very limited. She didn't know any of them well enough to surmise the best method of contact and how to go about it without Douglas getting wind of what she was up to. With no near family and no real friends, Teresa was her only hope. She had no choice but to give Teresa the file she was developing and trust her to somehow get it to the right people were she not to survive.

After an unusually quiet dinner, Rena arose from the table when her husband returned to his study. She stopped in the kitchen long enough to whisper in the cook's ear before going up to shower and prepare for bed. She studied her breast in the mirror. It was too tender to touch forcing her to dab carefully to dry off. Already there was a dark purple lump that was deep enough it would be slow to fade. Staring into her reflected image, she watched herself stand straight and stiffen her spine. Enough was enough. Somehow she would leave him and soon. It was late when Douglas came to bed. She forced herself to feign sleep as she prayed he would leave her alone. When he plopped onto the bed and prepared for sleep without reaching for her, it took all of her will power not to heave a sigh of relief. He was soon snoring off the effects of a copious quantity of scotch on top of the wine he had drunk at dinner. Sleep did not come for her; instead she looked back at her life and the route that led to her present circumstance.

Rena had grown up poor. Her father was an abusive

alcoholic and her mother as well.   With an agile brain and model looks, she had escaped as soon as she could and made her way to New York where she landed a job at the perfume counter of Bergdorf Goodman.   Even living in a cheap apartment and working for minimum wages was a step up for her and she was happy despite economic circumstances that allowed for nothing in the way of luxury.   When Douglas Forsyth came in to buy a bottle of Chanel perfume for his current girlfriend, he ended up buying it for Rena instead and taking her to dinner.   That was the beginning of a whirlwind courtship that introduced her to the glamour, excitement, and glitz of the high life.   From the first moment she was dazzled by this new world of opulence and privilege as much as she was by the handsome politician.   When he proposed she never stopped to ask if he was right for her or if she was in love.   At that moment she had blinders on that only allowed her to look straight ahead into a world she had never even dreamed of attaining.   Now that she was in it and surrounded by every luxury she wondered if it were worth the price of her own soul. Was anything worth that price?   Looking back she realized she had never known the man behind the carefully polished facade. Now that she saw him for what he was, she could only wonder how she could have been so willfully blind.   She had not protested when he began to control the way she dressed, where she went, and what she did.   She had not protested when he needlessly bumped her and caused her to stagger into something.   She had not protested the first slap or the first beating.   She had tolerated it all and it had only escalated to the point she now feared for her very life.

Once she had met Douglas, he had left the guy she had been

dating without looking back. She wondered if she had stayed with him if she would have children by now and a little cottage in the suburbs. Douglas had long avoided the issue of children saying that the time wasn't right for him and she was young enough that she had years ahead to be a mother. Perhaps, that life would have been a far richer, in all the ways that seemed to matter, but was now beyond her reach. The gray light of dawn was seeping through the crack in the drapes when she finally fell into fitful sleep.

Douglas left the bed without awakening her. Prior to coming to bed that night, he had sent an email to Paris from Tony the Tiger advising them to proceed with an alternate plan. He did not intend to go for the big goal until he was sure that he was not compromised. He had also decided to allow his wife to live for the time being. He wasn't in love with Rena, never had been, but it was easier to keep her than to look for a new wife he could train to the role he expected. He would tighten the screws on her freedom even beyond what it was currently. She would no longer be allowed to drive her car anywhere. If she wanted to go to a hair appointment or shopping, his chauffeur would dog her every step. As for the cook, he wasn't ready to lose her, but he would have her watched too, and he would stop the camaraderie his wife appeared to have developed with the black woman. His wife would not dare defy him. She was a weak, cowed woman and he intended to keep her that way.

Douglas called for his driver to take him to his office in the Longworth House Office building. He was speaking before congress later in the day and needed to work on his speech. Looking at his calendar he noted that his secretary had scheduled a formal reception at the Italian Embassy for eight that night. He instructed her to call his wife and let her know to dress appropriately. He kept a spare tux at the office so he would not need to go home. A driver would pick up Rena and bring her to the office as he was leaving. They would arrive together like the loving couple the public assumed them to be. It took him until noon to polish his speech. Glancing at the clock, he smiled. Things should be happening in Paris at that very moment if all went as planned.

He leaned back in his chair, propped his feet on the fine mahogany desk and picked up the television remote. Scrolling to CNN, he waited for the commercial to finish and news to resume. The talking head was going through a litany of trivial events when breaking news interrupted the feed. Douglas grinned with satisfaction. The screen was filled with running, screaming people, some covered in blood. The panicked announcer described a subway bombing near the Eiffel Tower and the number of injured and dead. While the count was not as high as he might have liked, it was a success and the owner of the deadly backpack had escaped. The police suspected a tie to ISIS and were establishing checkpoints at all possible avenues of escape from the city. They would not find the man. He was hiding in their ranks.

All had gone smoothly giving him the go-ahead to proceed with his big plans for Paris. Next he would devise a new event for London. He would watch President Northrup's campaign schedule for the next time the Vice-President and he were together. He had waited for years. A few more days were inconsequential. He clicked off the television and put on his jacket. He was having lunch at Old Ebbitt Grill with some of his colleagues who were supporting him in the introduction of a new bill to allow for more funding for immigrants from the ravaged Middle East. He was at his most convivial self during lunch. He had to stop himself from smirking at his gullible cohorts.

Chapter 14

A severe thunderstorm during the night knocked out electricity to the island. It was still out when the household began to stir. Jill rolled from the bed and tiptoed to the bathroom. It was not until she tried to turn on the light over the sink and nothing happened that she realized the power was out. She then tried the overhead light and with it out too, she figured the storm had shut down service to the house and perhaps the island. Walking over to the cell phone she had plugged in to charge, she picked it up intending to search for a number to call to report a power outage. When it did not come on, she walked over to her husband's phone that was charging on the opposite side of the bed. Its screen remained dark as well. Shaking her husband she told him what she had found. Gerald swore softly as he rose from bed.

"I'll check with Quint. I feel sure he mentioned a generator that kicks in when the power is interrupted. There must be something wrong with it or we would have some power."

"I sure hope you guys can get it running. I think I will let the boys sleep in a while longer. Maybe we will have electricity back on by the time they wake up."

At the knock on his door, Quint raised up on his elbows and called, "Come in." When he saw Gerald in the doorway, he asked, "What's up?"

"That storm last night was a humdinger. It knocked out the electricity and both Jill's cell phone and mine are dead. For some reason your generator didn't come on."

"Crap. I guess the Hendersons didn't live long enough to have another tank of fuel delivered. I noticed it was out when I was here. Sorry, I forgot all about it. I'll get dressed and run into town and see what I can do."

"Is your cell working?'

"It had a full charge so it should be fine. I have a couple of spares you can use that I keep charged. My laptop should be okay unless there was a huge power surge. How about yours?"

"Yeah, mine too. Want to call the power company to see when we can expect electric service to be back on?"

"I'm on it."

"Here, catch." Quint tossed him a spare phone. "Use it until you get another."

When Gerald left, Quint pulled on an old faded pair of jeans and his favorite T-shirt. Slipping on dock shoes, he put his wallet in his pocket. In the bedside drawer he found the emergency service number for Progress Energy and waited for an answer. A computerized voice told him that electrical service for the island should be on within the hour. With restoration expected shortly there was no need to make a mad dash for fuel for the generator. Instead he called the supplier and ordered enough for three days to prevent being caught short in the future. With that done, he dug around in the closet and pulled out his latest inspiration. When he open the bedroom door Code was waiting expectantly, his leash already in his mouth.

"Decided to check on me did you, you traitor? Don't you know you've got to stop abandoning me to sleep in the boys' room? I'm getting jealous." Code cocked his head at him and then bobbed it up and down as though he understood. Quint laughed as he snapped the leash onto the dog's collar. "Come on. Let's go to the beach and see if I can get these contraptions working while you chase birds and crabs."

Knocking at Gerald's door he called, "Power on within the hour."

"Great."

At the end of the walk, Quint sat down and picked up one of the small seagull looking drones he had programmed. Switching the first one on, he watched it lift into the air and begin a slow circle about 500 feet up. It was programmed to monitor anyone leaving the mainland by boat and heading on a trajectory toward his property. Equipped with a powerful camera and solar charged batteries, it would transmit images to his computer for up to twelve hours. Next he picked up the second of the drones and activated it. This one would fly in an oblong loop along the beach where anyone attempting to access the property from the beach would immediately be picked up and his computer alerted to the intrusion. With the team of agents the CIA had promised delayed on another op, it would be at least a day before he could rely on their backup. Quint figured the drones were a smart addition to any security plan as they would spot intruders well before anyone on the property could.

Watching the drones run their patterns, he used his big toes to push off first one shoe and then the other before walking down to where Code was chasing sand fiddlers along the shoreline. The damp sand felt as refreshing as a cold beer on a sweltering day. He loved the island in the morning quiet with the sound of the surf and the call of birds singing the eternal music of the coast. At times like this it was easy to forget all of the unpleasant things that exist in today's world and just glory in being alive. Code seemed to feel the same way as he capered about barking joyfully. Quint laughed with sheer pleasure. Picking up a scallop shell, he threw it and watched as Code set off to fetch. Hearing excited shouts, he looked over his shoulder to see two barefoot boys running lickidy-split across the sand to join him. Deciding to have some fun, he dug one of the controls from the pocket of his hoodie and switched it to manual. A drone came swooping down just above their heads when the boys were about three yards away. Ducking they looked up as the 'bird' make another dive toward them. Both boys began dancing with excitement when they realized that Quint was playing with them. Soon Code added his baying to their shouts, bringing Jill and Gerald to the end of the walk to seek the source of the uproar. Laughing at the antics and the excitedly leaping dog, they removed their own shoes and joined Quint and the boys'.

"Looks like you have a new toy," Gerald commented.

"Serious-business toy. This little birdie is state of the art surveillance. There's another one up there, too. I've programmed them both to keep an eye on things until we get some cover out here." Quint reset the control to the required pattern before pushing the return command. He didn't want to run down the batteries. He wanted full coverage for the coming night when the batteries would have to rely on the stored charge.

"Nice touch," again Gerald was surprised at the many facets of a man he was just beginning to know and appreciate. Both he and Quint reached up to capture the 'birds' as they flew in.

"Let me, let me!" both boys cried in unison.

Their Mom interrupted, "Sorry boy, these are men's toys and they won't even let me play with them. Why don't we all go up to the house and see what we can rustle up for breakfast? Do you have an iron skillet, Quint?"

"Yes, ma'am. All good southe'n' boys got them skillets," Quint drawled. "What you planning to do with it?"

"I thought if you big bruisers would fire up the grill we could have a breakfast picnic. How does that sound?"

"F...... ah, wonderful," Quint glanced at the kids; thankful he had caught himself in time to avoid the expletive.

Gerald snickered before he parroted, *"Yeah, f...... ah, wonderful!"*

Jill shook her head and muttered, "Clowns. I'm surrounded by children and clowns."

The jovial mood continued through an improvised picnic. Shortly afterwards the electricity came on and they made a tour of the house to see what had been damaged due to any power surge. The Internet modem had survived due to a transient voltage surge protector. The only damage on a cursory inspection appeared to be the Williams' cell phones that were not only dead but fried. Gerald solved that problem by calling the Wilmington branch of the agency and having two more delivered. They were there before noon. Both Quint and Gerald wasted no time getting onto their computers. Quint immediately went to the terrorist website and scrolled looking for recent postings. The one from Tony the Tiger leaped out at him. He jotted down the sequence of numbers and immediately began to decode.

Quint yelled, "Shit! Those mother fuckers."

"Hey, pipe down. I've got impressionable sons here."

"Sorry, Gerald. I just intercepted another message. We are too late to do anything about it. Turn on the television and see if there is anything on the news. If I am not mistaken, the Paris subway got hit this morning. Two dead and five injured due to a bomb in a backpack left on one of the trains."

"Hold on. An email just popped up from the Agency. They are confirming that. So what do you think?"

"I'm puzzled. It doesn't fit with the grandiose plans for London and Washington. I wonder if this could have been a fishing expedition to see after the failure in London and the reschedule in Washington whether or not we caught on to them. Maybe it's a good thing we were out of pocket; although I'm sure those victims in Paris wouldn't agree. I think maybe this was a test to see whether or not the code was compromised."

"That makes sense." Gerald tapped his pencil on his desk in a rapid staccato as he thought.

"What in the hell is that shit?"

"What shit?"

"The pencil tap. It's enough to drive me nuts."

"Sorry. Force of habit." Gerald dropped his pencil on his desk. "So what do you think is next?"

"I think there will shortly be another posting for something in Paris. Do you think you could arrange a fake joint appearance for POTUS and the Veep at some fundraiser? We can control that. As soon as I get a read on Paris and any planned event there, we can warn Interpol and the French. I have Lila working on a trace for the origin of this Tony the Tiger. I would damned well love to nail that Tiger asshole."

"Yeah, so would I." Gerald picked up the spare phone Quint had given him, "This secure?"

"It's good."

The minute his office picked up, Gerald gave rapid-fire instructions. Then he fell silent while he listened to whoever was on the other end. After several minutes Gerald exclaimed, "You're shitting me?"

"So, how bad is it?" Gerald asked. Quint turned to look at a man whose face had gone ashen. After several more minutes, Gerald said, "Okay, keep me posted on any change."

When he hung up, Quint asked, "What in the hell was that about, if I'm allowed to know?"

"The director had a heart attack. They don't know if he will make it. If he doesn't, I will be acting in his place for the interim. Shit. That means I have to get back to Washington. Then where does that leave my wife and kids?

"Your wife and kids are fine here...as safe as anywhere. You know I will stay with them if you have to leave. Just don't get ahead of yourself. Wait and see where this goes."

"You're right. I just never wanted to be the director. Even if it is interim, I don't want it."

"Don't decide right now. Just ride this out and see what develops. In the meantime, I intend to secure things here. I don't know if the bad guys are onto our whereabouts yet, but I plan to be prepared for them. If they come looking for trouble they are damned well going to find it."

"Anything I can do? "

"Hell, I'm not even sure what I'm going to do yet. Soon as I figure something out, I'll let you know."

"Fine. In the meantime, I need to answer about a million emails and get back to my guys to see what is happening with Doc Hollins and the search for his wife's killers."

"No problem. I'm going to take a little walk down the beach with Code and see what possibilities exist for trouble should it crop up. I would take the boys, but I don't want them to go that far until we get things secured."

"I'll have Jill distract them. If they see you and Code leaving, they'll have a fit to go too. Soon as Jill gets them occupied, hightail it out of here."

"Will do."

He watched the breakers rolling onto the sand until he heard Jill call the boys to the back of the house. Quint gave a low whistle and waited for Code to join him. He knew his dog was smart, but when he saw him walk up with his leash in his mouth, he decided Code was a mind reader as well. Quint scratched him behind his ears as he snapped the leash into place. He murmured, "Good boy."

His first order of business was to check the neighboring houses to see if anyone was in residence. He started with the two on the immediate right. The first one belonged to a retired CEO of a Fortune 500 company. He had met the man and his wife while his parents were still alive. When he knocked on the door, Carole Levinworth greeted him and invited him into the family room where Bob Levinworth was watching the morning news. He arose when they entered.

"Quint Cord. Boy, I haven't seen you in a coon's age." They shook hands and Bob motioned him to be seated.

Carole offered him a cup of coffee that he declined.

"I'm fine, thanks. I just wanted to drop by and let you know that I'm home in case you see lights and wonder who's there."

Bob shook his head, "That was a sad business with the Hendersons. They were fine people and we have missed having them around. Do you know who would do such a thing?"

"Not yet. It's still under investigation."

"I know we will be happy when they catch whoever did it. Carole and I haven't been comfortable since. Something like that has never before happened here. One reason we moved here is because of the limited access. It made us feel safe. Now, I'm not sure we ever will feel that way again."

They chatted for a few more minutes before Quint excused himself. The neighboring house belonged to a young couple that he knew only by rumor. Both were doctors in a renal clinic on Military Highway. When he rang the bell, a nanny opened the door. She held an infant in her left arm, while in her right hand a toddler was struggling to free himself from her grasp. Quint introduced himself and asked her to pay his respect to the couple. Walking down the steps of the Florida style mansion, he made his way back to the hard-packed sand along the shore and walked back past the imposing Levinworth house and then his own before walking up to the house on the opposite side. The Stanfield couple was not at home but he could hear a dog barking inside. Slipping his card in the door, he went down their steps and walked along the street to the next house.

The Georgian mansion belonged to another retired couple that had been good friends of his parents. Quint liked them both. A maid answered the door and when he explained who he was, she invited him in.

"Mr. Andrews is not feeling well this morning and is still in bed. I hate to wake him up. His wife went to some kind of charity luncheon but should be back by two, if you want to come by later."

"I'll try to do that. Just let them know that I'm at home so if they see the house is occupied, they don't need to be alarmed."

"We are all really sorry about the Hendersons. I hope they find who was responsible for such a horrible thing."

"Thank you. So do I."

Chapter 15

Gerald, newly appointed director of the CIA, sat across the conference table from the President, his cabinet, and congressional leaders. He did not want to be there and he did not want the job. President Northrup had given him little option. Gerald noted the tired features of the President and figured he had slept little the night before as he dealt with the CIA leadership crisis. The man had aged more than most in the position he held, perhaps due to an ever-greater threat to the Western World from the infiltration of determined Jhadists. Attacks had increased in Europe with the latest atrocity killing nearly five hundred at a stadium in Marseilles. Another three hundred had lost their lives at a concert in London. In the States, the last three attacks totaled six hundred and fifty dead and scores more grievously wounded. The public was baying for action but no one could decide how to find the proverbial needles in a haystack. Tolerant immigration policies for refugees had led to an untold number of terrorists gaining a toehold in Western countries. Attempts to enact legislation to rout them out died in Congress for fear some would label it profiling and discriminatory. While hearts bled symbolically for the flight of the refugees, real blood was running in the streets of the Western World.

Watching the President, Gerald noted a slight tremor in his right hand. Had it not been for his training it was subtle enough he would not have noticed. No one else seemed to have observed it. The tick in the lid of the man's right eye added to the impression of someone under stress.   In three years President Northrup's hair had turned white and his skin had faded from a deep golden tan to the pallor of clabbered milk. Lines carved grooves in a face that had been relatively youthful prior to stepping into the most powerful office in the world. Once a successful businessman who had reached that stage in life when he could have retired to some island paradise, Clayton Northrup instead had chosen to dedicate his remaining years to trying to save the country he loved from misguided politicians who refused to look beyond the next election cycle. Substantial opposition   in   the   legislature   made   the   job   almost insurmountable. Only his innate charm allowed him to tread a precarious path in order to push a goodly number of the changes he espoused through the hostile ranks of Congress. Gerald shrugged his shoulders and forced himself to pay attention to the mild objections raised by a couple of Congressmen to his appointment to Thomas's post.   The President ignored them as he continued on with his reasons for naming Gerald to the vacant position.   Studying the faces around the table, he knew some of them were remembering his appearance before the Congressional committee when he had taken the fall for the Agency.

*****

Marshall Thomas had died the night before, at about the same time Gerald was inquiring at the information desk of the hospital for his room number. He had shown his badge to the security agent stationed outside Thomas's room. Seeing the door partially closed, he knocked. When there was no answer, he looked in and saw Thomas lying on the bed hooked up to monitors. As he stood there, hesitating to enter further, a nurse pushed past him and dashed to the bed. Checking for a pulse, she looked up at him and asked, "Are you family?"

"An associate." He looked at the way the nurse was disconnecting the monitors and it suddenly registered, "Is he dead?"

"Yes, sad to say. I heard the emergency alarm sound at the station, but I couldn't get here quickly enough as I was with another patient."

"Is it too late to try the electric shock paddles?"

"I'm sorry. He specifically forbade any and all interventions even had I come the moment the alarm sounded. Now, if you will excuse me, I need to call the doctor and notify his wife."

Gerald looked at the man's face just before the nurse pulled the sheet over him. He could not remember it ever looking so peaceful. For a moment, remorse overcame him when he recalled all of the times Marshall Thomas had angered him. The job was high intensity, a political minefield, and filled with budgetary and political frustrations. And, that did not even touch the very real issues critical to national security that crossed his desk daily. In hindsight, he knew he could have been more charitable to a man with that kind of daily stress. He murmured, "rest in peace, Mr. Thomas." As for him, he suspected his days had just become far less peaceful.

Early that morning a six o'clock call awakening him from a fretful sleep confirmed his fears. When he hung up, he stretched his arms above his head and stumbled to the bath in his office. The sofa that he had spent the night on was too short, causing him to sleep in a curled position. Definite twinges of pain in his back, convinced him that the Agency office was not a viable housing solution, despite reluctance to return home until he knew who was trying to get to him and his family. He brushed his teeth, took a quick shower, and rummaged in the closet until he came up with a clean shirt. He put on his tie and adjusted it as he stared in the mirror. He looked like hell. Even a quick brush of his hair didn't help the fact there were bags under his eyes. He shook his head. Despite the constant threats he had faced working in the field, the stress and inertia of a desk job brought its own ravages to the body. While not as immediately deadly, it was a slow decline in stamina and physical health. He promised to find time to use the company gym to work out in his non-existent spare time.

Gerald had glanced at his watch, and groaned. If he wanted to be on time for the meeting with the President he was going to have to haul ass.

*****

That had been three hours ago. And now he was officially the new director. He looked around the room at the serious faces and felt a cold sweat break out. God alone knew what his acceptance of the position would bring into his life. Gerald rubbed his sweaty palms on his pants legs. The meeting was winding down and he could tell by the folders being neatly closed that everyone was waiting for the President's dismissal. When Northrup stood and extended his hand, Gerald took it. He looked into the man's eyes and saw a brief glimpse of compassion for the task ahead before a shutter dropped and once again the Commander in Chief was all business.

"Director Williams, we appreciate the service you have rendered in the past and look forward to this new relationship. I don't need to impress upon you the seriousness of the office to which you have been assigned. More than anyone else in here, I am sure you know. I want to assure you that anytime you need to speak to me, you may call the number in the folder there and you will reach me directly without having to go through channels."

Gerald nodded his thank you as the President continued, "Gentlemen, thank you for rearranging your schedules to be here this morning. I want to reiterate our gratitude to Director Williams and assure him that we are all on the same team."

"Thank you sir, gentlemen. I am honored by the confidence you have placed in me. If it is in my power, I will never let you down."

For a wild moment Gerald hope that Congress would reject the nomination and he could go back to a relatively peaceful life, but he knew that was a futile hope. With the backing of the powerful men in the room and the President, a Congressional vote was mere procedural protocol. His Nation had called him to service and he would serve to the best of his ability. He had worked indirectly with the DNI director, Victor Erickson, for the last two years and knew him to be a fair man. He glanced across at Erickson, his new boss, who caught his eye and nodded in approbation. Allowing his eyes to roam around the table Gerald felt that they were all pulling for him except for perhaps Forsyth. He had never trusted the man.

As if hearing his thoughts, Douglas Forsyth leaned across the table and shook Gerald's hand, "I know you will do a fine job, Director. If I can ever be of help, let me know. Unlike some in government, I respect and defend the CIA and all you do to keep us safe."

"Thank you, sir. I appreciate that." Forsyth left the room after shaking the hands of those remaining and murmuring the expected replies, Gerald left as well. He wanted nothing so much as a stiff shot of whiskey even though he had not yet had breakfast. He chuckled. If he gave into that urge under stress he would soon be an alcoholic.

Forsyth was waiting for him at the elevator. "Allow me to treat you to brunch. The Congressional dining room does a fine one."

Wondering at the friendliness of a man that had never bothered to speak to him before, Gerald nodded his head in agreement. "Sure. I think I have time."

At the moment the omelet he had ordered was placed on the table in front of him, Gerald's office was busy gathering the latest information on his secretary's murder to present to him. He put aside wondering what was happening at the office. That was not the immediate concern as he tried to figure exactly what Douglas Forsyth was fishing for. And fishing he was. Not only did the 'what' concern him, but even more important to know was the 'why.'

"Congressman Forsyth, I appreciate your concern for security implications at the unfortunate demise of my secretary and assure you we are looking at every angle to ascertain whether or not some hostile operative might have been using her for insider information. At this point, we have no reason to believe it was anything more than some sadistic, murdering rapist that killed her." Gerald looked down at his plate and sliced off a bite of sausage that he stuffed into his mouth and began chewing. He wanted time to think and he was not ready to reveal any of his suspicions regarding Marlowe's death to anyone, and especially not Forsyth. He studied the powerful legislator as he pretended to eat his meal. Gerald suspected the congressman had already eaten judging by the man's obvious lack of appetite. He could only conclude that either he wanted information that had not yet been released, or he was simply trying to curry favor. Gerald had never liked the bastard and was disinclined to give him anything. He well remembered the congressional hearing when Douglas had joined those aggressively baying for his ass. That was one more reason why something didn't ring right about the man's sudden friendliness.

Gerald put his fork and knife on his plate, blotted his mouth, and laid his napkin on the table. "I appreciate the meal, sir. I was just about starved as I'd eaten nothing since lunch yesterday."

"No problem. Think nothing of it. I'm just glad we had an opportunity to get to know one another a little better." Douglas paused before smiling disarmingly. He continued, "I hope you won't hold that little Congressional hearing into CIA activities against me. I know you took some heat, but it was never directed at you, you understand?"

"Of course, not. Think nothing of it, sir." Gerald rose, "If you will excuse me, I really need to get back to Langley and figure out how to fill Thomas's shoes."

"Fine, fine. You call me, now, if you ever need any help on The Hill. Like I said, I have always supported the CIA."

"Will do."

Gerald shook hands with Douglas and hurried from the dining room.

It was all he could do not to wipe his palm on his pants on the way out. He had always considered the man an oily bastard and that hadn't changed. One brunch was not going to erase years of animus. On the way out, Gerald telephoned to have his car waiting at the building's rear entrance. With that done, he scrolled through his contact list and hit the latest telephone number for Quint. He needed to let him know what was happening and to check on his wife and kids.

Quint picked up on the first ring. "I saw the news on television. So, I guess I should call you Director Williams now."

Gerald groaned, "Screw that. Let's keep it to Gerald. I guess I'm stuck with the job though. The President didn't give me any wiggle room. After that Congressional hearing several years ago I thought I would be lucky to be a janitor in the CIA offices. I never dreamed I would end up as its director."

"That is what is going to make you a good one. You're not a greedy, narcissistic SOB that just wants to climb the power ladder in D.C. At any rate, congratulations...I guess."

"Yeah...I guess." Gerald made the turn into Langley as he asked, "How is my family?"

"They're all fine. Right now they're making happy with your guys. Buster, and a couple of his men came in earlier. The kids think we imported some grown up playmates, so they are happy as clams. Jill's just glad I'm helping with the cooking so she doesn't have to feed them all without any assistance. They eat like they're starved for some home cooking. Actually, I suspect they probably are. Two agents from the Wilmington office are providing rotating backup and they have the Coast Guard lined up to monitor any shore-to-island traffic during the night. I've got my drones doing their job and Buster has his guys monitoring from the cupola. I think it's covered and we always have the safe room if necessary. Everything is quiet so far."

"I hope the hell it stays that way."

"So do I. You want to talk to Jill?"

"Yeah, and she's not going to be happy I accepted the directorship. Move any valuable stuff away from her when you give her the phone. I wouldn't want her to be tempted to throw some treasure of yours."

Both men laughed at the absurdity of the pragmatically calm woman throwing a temper tantrum. Her tongue and wit were all the weapons she needed. After Gerald hung up with his wife who was less than pleased, but thankfully understanding, he called his office to have ready a full report on the Hollins woman, any information obtained from the interrogation of Abdul, and from the terrorist's cell phone Quint had brought from London. In less than ten minutes he was walking through the office door to a chorus of congratulations. News traveled fast in the Washington grapevine.

Gerald sat at his old desk and surveyed the waiting stacks of folders, all marked confidential or classified. Until they removed all personal effects from the director's office, he would stay in his old one. The few days it would take to make the transition from his office to one a floor up suited him just fine. He liked his old space, maybe more than the one he would move to. It wasn't as nice, but he loved the view from the window and the office had grown as comfortable as an old pair of shoes. He picked up the photograph of his wife and kids and smiled. He was glad they were out of the city and as safe as he could make them. Now that he was director, there would be some adjustments to make. They would need a new house equipped with special security, bulletproof windows, accommodations for a security detail, a safe room, and special alarms and sensors. Their current house was too small and not adaptable. He smiled. Quint could give the agency lessons on some of that. He also would have to adapt to a driver carting him around everywhere and the ever-hovering presence of guards. He was going to hate the lack of privacy. He suspected that aspect of the job would drive Jill nuts. He put the photo back in its usual spot on the left side of his desk, and paged his new secretary to come in.

Brenda Sue Rawlings walked into the office, shut the door behind her and waited to be summoned forward. She was nervous. He could tell by the way she shifted her eyes to the chair and then back to him, stutter-stepped with indecision, and then stopped. He pointed to the chair and watched her sink into it, carefully pulling her skirt down to modestly cover her knees...no mean feat considering the brevity of it. Her struggles with a skirt that refused to stay down reminded him of the window shade in his room when he was a kid. He would pull it down and release it just right so it would go pinging back up ending with a satisfying slapping sound. He shook the memory from his head and plunged in with a rapid-fire list of instructions. First on the list was an emphasis on total secrecy and constant caution to assure security; second was to contact the group assigned to finding and adapting housing for officials in need of special protection. He continued with the list ending with how he liked his coffee. He watched her making careful notes as he talked. While not as attractive as Marlowe, all that mattered to him was whether or not Brenda Rawlings would be both efficient and trustworthy. Time would tell he supposed. When he was finished, he thanked her. As she closed the door on leaving, he picked up the top folder in the stack. It was going to be a long day.

Chapter 16

Douglas Forsyth was worried. Not because of the brunch...it had gone better than he expected. Gerald Williams seemed amenable and accessible, not like the previous Director with whom he had locked horns on numerous occasions. He decided he would cultivate the relationship with Williams. The question was what he could do that would assure the man's loyalty. At the moment, the biggest concern in his mind was whether or not the three men he sent to take out Williams and his family had been killed in the process or taken captive. If taken captive, he had to decide if there was any way to trace them back to him. The other outstanding problem was Abdul's failure. None of the four operatives' bodies had been found, or at least nothing had appeared in the news to that effect, nor had there been anything on the two attacks against the Williams family. Either all had been killed or some had been taken captive and were being interrogated. He had to be careful pointing the finger at the Saudis due to his relationship with Prince Fayed. Thus the question became on whom he should focus the blame in order to deflect any trace back to him should the need arise. Perhaps, he should call them some kind of terrorist cell that resented Williams from his time in the field when he had been active in taking down several members of the Taliban. Whatever he did, he was removing any hit on Williams from his list. He wanted a door into the CIA and with that bitch Marlowe out, he no longer had an inside source.

Then there was the issue of Marlowe. He had no way of

knowing if she had spilled her guts to her husband. That was another problem he needed to think about. He was rapidly running out of operatives to call on to fix his problems. So far the only ones left were Jamil and Mohammed, the two that eliminated the Hollins woman. He decided to have a little fishing expedition before he pulled the plug on the doctor. If Dr. Hollins knew nothing, it was better to leave him alone. An attack on her husband, as well, would assure that the CIA would not buy a rape story.

The biggest concern facing him was eliminating the Republican President and Vice President. As Speaker of the House he would step in almost a year before the end of their term. A grateful Nation would then substitute him in the race for President instead of one of the weakest Democrats to run in a long time. The frontrunner and certain nominee, Democratic Senator Vance of Nevada, had a history of blood clots and a previous mild stroke. At seventy years of age, the overweight Vance was far from the prime of health. His tendency to fudge on the truth to deflect attention from his weaknesses verged on the blatantly obvious. That coupled with questionable financial dealings, and an arrogant and remote attitude, further lessened his appeal to the general public. Furthermore, Forsyth had studiously cultivated a close relationship with the DNC chairman, Rickie Nash. He could depend on her support in a move to dump Vance. If need be, Vance could have an accident or some unfortunate illness. Such things were not that difficult to arrange.

France needed to be dealt with as well. He expected his informants there to have a new schedule in his hands within a few days. The only other problem was keeping the Prince happy after a series of non-events, instead of the calamitous happenings the Saudi had expected from plots designed to throw three preeminent western nations into turmoil. Talking to the Prince was not wise until he had accomplished at least one of the objectives. After the money the man had put up, with little to show for it except the peripheral and meaningless bombing in Paris, the Prince would be pissed.

Forsyth pushed back from his desk enough to prop his feet on the edge and leaned back in his chair. The wheels in his head kept turning as he tried to figure out the next step. This time there could be no mistakes. Things had to go right. He was jarred from his thoughts by an insistent buzzing. Cursing, he dropped his feet to the floor and reached for the button, snapping, "Yes?"

His secretary, Sarah Stanley, waited for him to berate her for interrupting him. She held her breath for a beat to give him time to start in on her. When he did not, she said, "I'm sorry, sir. Prince Fayed is on the phone and asked to speak to you. What should I tell him?"

"Fuck." He had no intention of taking that call until he had decided how best to deal with the failures that had occurred. He snarled, "Tell him that I am out of the office for the day in an important meeting with the President and that I cannot be interrupted. I'll try to call him tomorrow."

"Yes. Is that all?"

His answer was the click of the receiver in her ear. She muttered under her breath *mean old bastard*, before relaying Forsyth's message to the irate Prince.

Fayed swore in Arabic before saying, "Please tell him for me that I strongly suggest he call me as soon as possible."

"Of course, your highness. I am so sorry I am unable to reach him immediately."

Before she could return to her typing, the inner office door banged open and Forsyth stalked out. "What did he say?"

She watched his face turn red with anger as she relayed the message.

"Bastard. Who does that fucker think he is to tell me what to do?" The Speaker rubbed his face before barking, "I'm out for the rest of the afternoon. Take any calls. Put the names and messages in a memo and email them to me before you leave."

She watched him walk out the door before sticking out her tongue at his retreating back. It may have been childish, but she he couldn't stand the man and it made her feel better to express it in some way. However, she needed the job and until another opening came up she was stuck. She was tempted to spend the remainder of the day updating her résumé but with a stack of paperwork to deal with she did not have that option.

As she was shutting down her computer for the day, her phone rang. Damn, she had hoped to get away early for once. Suppressing her irritation, she assumed her best professional voice.

"Speaker Forsyth's office. May I help you?"

"And you are?"

"This is his secretary, Sarah Stanley."

Gerald Williams exclaimed, "Wonderful, just the one I wanted to talk to. I'm Gerald William, director of the CIA following the recent death of Director Thomas. But, announcing that is not the reason for my call. As you may have heard, my secretary was killed a few days ago."

"I did hear that. What an awful tragedy." Surely the new

head of the CIA was not calling just to tell her his secretary was dead. For a wild moment she wondered if perhaps he wanted her to fill the vacancy. That thought was put to rest when he continued.

"Yes, it was terrible. The reason I ask is because a trace on her phone calls shows numerous ones from your office leading me to think that perhaps the two of you were close friends."

"I'm sorry, but I never knew her. I don't recall placing any calls to your office, sir. I think Speaker Forsyth called the former Director a number of times, but that is all I can remember. Should I ask the Speaker about it?"

"May I call you Sarah?"

"Of course, if you wish."

"Thanks, Sarah. As a government employee you are aware of the importance of a request for secrecy, therefore do not mention my call to anyone? I do not wish to involve the Speaker in CIA business. He is a busy man and does not need to be informed. It is critical that you honor my request, regardless, to keep this between us. Do you understand?"

"Absolutely. I won't tell a soul." She stared at the receiver after he hung up wondering what that was all about. Shrugging her shoulders, she collected her things and went home to a quiet dinner in front of the television with her cat curled up beside her. Her day had been long. Soon the phone call was far from her mind.

*****

That was not the case with Gerald. Glancing at the clock on the far wall he saw that it was almost ten. He had finished the stack of correspondence on his desk and answered anything that was urgent. The call log kept nagging at him. He had never had a call from the Speaker, so why the repeated calls to his office? If they had been about a government issue, why had Forsyth not been put through to him? Was there some relationship to Forsyth that he did not know about? As he sat there pondering, it came to him. He fished Marlowe's unfinished letter from the file and read through it again. She had stopped just as she was about to divulge the name of the person blackmailing her. What if Forsyth knew about her background; maybe he had been involved with her sexually? Could he be the one responsible for her death when he realized he was losing control of his plant in the CIA? Furthermore, the log showed he had called her the day before she disappeared. Now, what could Gerald do to prove a connection?

Gerald tapped his pencil on his desk in rapid staccato. Abdul had been useless in divulging who had hired him. He had died of his injuries within a day of his capture and pain-killing drugs had rendered him insensate much of the time. Could Forsyth be responsible for the attacks on him and his family? Was he responsible for the attacks on Quint and Abdul's attack on Jeffrey to stop them from breaking the code? If that were the case, then there was a strong possibility he was the one behind the Tiger's Code. If he could find the perps that had murdered Marlowe and take them alive, he would have a path to the person who had hired them. Tracking them would therefore be his first order of business. The second would be to bug Forsyth's home and office and put him under surveillance. The second would take some time, as he would have to persuade the Attorney General to file a request with the FISA court and then await their decision. He also needed to find out where the funding was originating that hired the thugs in the recent incidents. Forsyth had money, but not the kind it took to run this kind of operation. Getting a warrant on the Speaker without some substantial facts to support his suspicions would prove problematic. He needed someone to hack into the Speaker's banking trail and leave no trace. The Agency had some of the world's best hackers on staff, but he was not sure he wanted to use them on something this sensitive. Frequently someone in the government, with a bone to pick or for whatever reason, leaked secrets into the Washington grapevine. And one this juicy would be hard to resist.

He worked until almost eleven. Taking a chance that Quint would still be up, he called his cell phone.

Cord answered on the first ring, "Hey, what's happening in Washington?"

"You don't want to know. Let's just say I'm up to my neck in alligators and swimming like hell. How is it going there?"

"Quiet. The kids are in bed. Jill said she was going to the bedroom to watch the news. Buster and his guys are either on duty or crashed in the Hendersons' cottage. The guy in the cupola has a thermos of coffee and is trying to stay awake. My drones are circling. The coast guard is circling. It is a calm and peaceful as paradise can be when its been invaded by an army of hot shots. At least 'paradise' is what Buster calls it. He says he isn't taking any more assignments from you unless they are here. I'm beginning to wonder how I'll pry him and his boys out when this is over. They are in pig heaven, man."

"I can't say that I blame them. I wish I were there, too. Unfortunately, I'm stuck here for the foreseeable future." Gerald paused, "By the way, any posts from Tony the Tiger?"

"Nothing so far. The minute there is I'll let you know."

"Quint, I have a question for you. Judging from your computer set-up which our boys still can't hack, I have to wonder how you did it."

"Well, that's refreshing to know."

Gerald ignored the sarcasm and waited.

Quint answered him, "I didn't. A friend of mine is a genius at that kind of thing. She did it for me. Why do you ask?"

"I need a hacker outside of the agency to do a little work for me. If she can stop something from being hacked, do you think she could reverse it and hack into someone else?"

"I know she can." Quint chuckled. She had hacked into Gerald's computer for him long before he had told him his real name. When 'G' had assigned the Tiger's case to him he felt he had a right to know the name of the man who would be pulling his strings.

"Why are you laughing?"

"Trust me, you do not want to know." Quint stared out the window at the moonlight glinting off the sea, "You want me to ask her if she would like a little sideline work?"

"That would be great but, Quint, don't tell her too much until she opts in. I'll handle it from there. Okay?"

"Sure. No problem."

"I'd better hang up with you and call my wife. Hopefully things will stay safe there."

"Hey man, I know you're worried about your family but they're fine and having a super good time. I don't mind having them here. It's good company for me after years of being alone. Besides, I can work from anywhere really and I love it here, too. You have a great wife and kids. I have to stop myself from chasing your wife and persuading her to leave your ass. I like her cooking and her looks are mighty appeal, too."

"Hey, hot shot, you don't go threatening the new boss of the CIA. I am an officially bad dude now."

"Don't I know it? Besides, she's crazy in love with you for some reason. You're going to have to tell me how a dull fellow like you managed that?"

"Piss off, Quint." Gerald laughed along with him. "I'd better call Jill while she's still awake and immune to your charms. Goodnight, and keep me posted."

"You got it."

Chapter 17

"So, where in the hell have you been and why should I do you any favors, piss-ant?"

There was no need to translate her mood, as she wasted no time in subtleties. The minute Quint said hello, Lila launched into him, her voice rising in octaves and volume by the second as she built up steam. "Do you realize how long it has been since I have heard from you? Have you any idea I just might have worried a wee little bit, you self-centered asshole?"

"Whoa, whoa, whoa, Lila. I couldn't call you sooner. It would have been too dangerous for both of us..."

"What in the hell do you mean 'both of us? What have you done that *I* am involved?"

"Babe, you are not involved in my mess except indirectly. I was afraid someone really bad might track my phone calls. The only one I have called since I skipped out is a guy in the CIA."

"The CIA! What in the shit are you up to?"

"I can't tell you that. The reason I called is to ask if you would be willing to use your computer skills to help some folks I know. They are really impressed with the stuff you set up for me."

"What kind of folks? The kind that can get me killed?" Her voice was skeptical and a little too soft for Quint's comfort.

"Babe, anything you can do might save a lot of people from getting killed. I think you will be safe as there is no need for anyone that might be a problem to know who you are. And, if you still care, it just might save your boyfriend's life."

"Oh, you know my boyfriend?" she asked sarcastically. "Gee, I didn't think anyone knew him."

"Hey, that's not fair. I told you a long time ago there are certain things I can't talk about. And yes, I consider myself your boyfriend. I don't want anyone else, in case you are wondering. I've missed you Lila. I would have called if I could. I just need you to trust me on this. Now, is it okay if I give your name to someone that could use your special brand of expertise?"

"Depends."

Quint took a deep breath before answering. "On what?"

Lila cooed, "On just how sorry you are for neglecting me. On when you are going to bother to see me again."

"You have no idea how much I would like to be with you right now."

"Prove it," she challenged.

On a sudden impulse he asked, "Look, today's Friday. Could you drive down to Wilmington for the weekend? I have a place on Figure Eight. It's kind of crowded at the moment, but my suite is private."

It was several seconds before she answered. Quint had begun to sweat and was beginning to regret asking. He really didn't want to lose her. This time she might finally have had enough to drop him for someone more attainable. He did not realize he had been holding his breath. At her response he dared to let it out.

"I can be there by eight tonight. Give me directions. And yeah, tell your friend to call me before five."

"Great. I'll see you then."

The expectant gleam in Jill's eyes had not vanished since Quint told her that he had a lady friend coming for the weekend. Whenever he caught her looking at him, she quickly turned her head away to hide the smirk. Finally, he could stand it no more.

"Okay, okay. So why are you looking at me like that?"

"Like what, Quint?"

"Don't play coy. You know what I mean."

"I'm not being coy at all. I'm just a little surprised that a confirmed bachelor like you has a lady friend to invite down for the weekend. Since you didn't mention freshening up one of the extra bedrooms, I have to assume she is a really close friend." Jill winked and then smiled as she waited for his response.

"You think you are so smart. But, yeah, she's a really close friend."

"Good for you!"

"Don't go planning the wedding, Jill. We are a long way from there."

"So what is she like to capture an elusive bachelor like you?"

"I never said I was captured." Quint laughed before continuing. "She is smart as they come and sassier than the law should allow."

"She sounds perfect. I think I'm going to like her."

Soon Quint would have no reason to doubt that. After the initial all around introductions the two women vanished into the kitchen. Following a dinner of shrimp and grits, an arugula salad, herb and garlic toasted bread, and a crisp chardonnay, both women worked together clearing the dishes and getting the excited twins in bed. Buster and the others had either gone to bed or were on duty. Quint sat alone on the deck watching the moonlight glinting on the waves and thinking about Lila. Afterwards the kids were settled, the two women joined him on the deck for an after dinner limoncello. They were so caught up in conversation with one another he suddenly felt left out.

As though sensing his mood, Lila leaned over and kissed him on the cheek. "Quint you should have introduced me to your friends long ago." She grinned at him and then winked at Jill, before continuing, "They almost make you seem human."

"Well, that's a hell of an endorsement!"

Jill interrupted the response she could see forming on Lila's lips, "You two love birds can fight this one out without me. I'm going to go call my husband and tell him goodnight before I tuck myself in."

Quint laughingly remarked, "Good riddance. At least you know when to make scarce."

Jill smirked, "As do you, darling. As do you."

Lila watched Jill as she disappeared into the house. "She's fabulous. I like her so much. I feel as though I have known her forever."

"Yes, she's terrific. I like her, too. I'm glad the two of you hit it off. It could have been uncomfortable otherwise."

"For sure, especially since I am now working for her husband. Mr. Williams and I had a long talk this afternoon. As soon as I get security clearance, he is sending me all of the emails to his former secretary that originated from Senator Forsyth's office along with any from a 'Tony the Tiger' character. He'll probably want you to give me any that you have as well. I am supposed to track all emails back to their origin."

"No problem. I doubt I have any that Gerald doesn't, but as soon as he give me the go-ahead you can have them. I want this asshole that killed my caretakers worse than you can know."

Lila's eyes widened with shock, "What are you talking about?"

"You may have seen in the news that an elderly couple was killed here a few weeks ago."

"Oh, my God! You mean they worked for you?"

Quint told her the story of the Hendersons and what they had meant to him and why he suspected they were murdered. When he was finished, Lila reached over and took his hand. She said nothing as she continued to stroke it. He leaned back in his chair and watched the breakers roll to shore. Words were not needed. For the first time he could feel an acceptance of the deaths and a lifting of his own guilt in them.

After a time, he lifted her hand to his lips and kissed it. "Thanks for coming, Lila, and not giving up on me. I really do care about you. Enough that it scares me for you and what I may be getting you into."

"I don't need you to tell me what to get into. I got into this all by myself. Hey, I'm a patriot, too. If I can help take down a few bad guys by doing what I do best, I'm all for it. Gerald Williams told me the risks, so I'm not blind. Somehow I trust him, and I trust you to look out for me. You damned well better, lover boy."

Standing, Quint pulled her up by her hand. "I think we need to get to bed now so I can start some of that looking after you. But, don't plan on sleeping. It's been too damned long, Lila!"

"Jeez, I thought you'd never ask."

The sun was just rising when they finally rolled in opposite directions, fluffed their pillows and sank into replete and exhausted oblivion. It was almost noon when they emerged from the bedroom to find fresh coffee and newly warmed croissants awaiting them. Jill was in her swimsuit and both boys were hopping up and down with impatience. Excusing herself once they were settled at the table, Jill gave them a knowing wink before taking her sons by the hand and leading them down to the beach with Code joyfully leaping by their side. When they had finished eating, Quint gathered the dishes, rinsed them, and stacked them in the dishwasher while Lila leaned on the granite counter enjoying another cup of coffee

"Why don't you get on your suit and join them, Lila. I need to take care of some business and then I'll come."

"Will do. Besides, I think my poor used body needs some down time."

"And you think mine doesn't?" Quint winked and then wiggled his brows suggestively, "Of course, I do recover fast."

"Slow down, lover boy. I'm off to the beach."

"Party pooper!"

"Nah, just upping the anticipation."

Watching her deliberately wiggle her ass at him as she left the room, he figured the anticipation had already begun. Shaking his head to clear the memory of the previous night, he walked to his computer and logged on. After checking for any emails that he needed to react to, Quint went to the guesthouse in search of Buster for a recon report. He arrived to find it deserted. Glancing out the repaired living room window he could see Buster and one of his men had joined the two women and kids. The women were stretched out on deckchairs with the men squatted in the sand by them watching the kids building a sandcastle. As he squinted against the sun's glare, Lila stood and walked over to the kids and began helping them build. When Buster walked over to join her, Quint felt the hard bite of jealousy. She was a desirable woman and he could not blame Buster for being interested, but dammit, Lila was his.

As soon as he could get to his room and change, he would be on his way to join the others. He had almost reached the door when his phone rang. Looking out he could see Buster and Lila with their heads together laughing. He was tempted not to answer, but when he saw the caller ID, he figured he had no choice.

"Jesus, you have impeccable timing," he growled.

"Good grief, Quint!" Gerald exclaimed. "What are you so ill about?"

"Aw, nothing, nothing. What's up?"

"Your girl Lila checked out, so send her any emails you have that might be pertinent. I already sent a bunch for her to get on. With some cross triangulations I'm hoping she can trace them back to the source. I also have her working on Forsyth's banking relationships to see if she can find the funding source. Sooner or later, we're going to nail this asshole."

"You seem pretty certain he's the one?"

"He's a strong possibility, but until we have something definite to go on anything is possible." Gerald paused, "I'm hoping my new position will give me a little more protection for me and my family. As soon as I can get a house that has the necessary security features, I want to bring Jill and the kids home. I hope you don't mind if we impose on you a little longer?"

"No way! I'm loving it. But, you may want to call Buster on back before he steals Lila." Quint wanted to bite his tongue off the minute it slipped out, but it was too late to stop the roar of laughter that followed.

"Man! I thought you were the cool bachelor sworn to elude the love trap. Guess I figured you wrong again."

"Shit. It's not that. I just hate involving people in my fucked up life. Look what happened to the Hendersons. Look how you feel about your own family. Tell me you aren't terrified all the time? I just don't know if I can deal with it."

For a long moment Gerald was silent. "If I told you it was easy, I'd be lying my ass off. Hell yes, I worry. But someone has to do this job. I happen to think that the security and well being of this Nation is worth a little discomfort on my part." He goaded Quint by adding, "If you don't feel that way and want out, I have another code breaker on tap. He's not as good or as intuitive as you, but he's good."

Quint could not quell the annoyance in his voice. "Get off it. I'm not going anywhere and you know it. I feel as strongly about what we are doing and the importance of it as you do. If I thought I couldn't cut it, I'd say so."

"Cool it. I'm just saying we don't own you. You are a talented man and you know I don't want to lose you. In fact, I'm looking to maybe expand your job description."

"At the moment, it's expanded about enough, thank you. Now, if you're through with me, I'm going to go punch Buster for flirting with my girl."

"Well, if he switches to Jill, punch him again for me."

"With pleasure. Later." Quint clicked off his phone and grabbed his sunglasses. Catching the thunderous expression on his face reflected in the window, he took a deep breath and counted to ten. He did not need Lila getting any ideas about wedding bells. He still had to figure out how to deal with the reality of the depth of the feelings for her that he had only just begun to realize. The question was what was he going to do about it. Always before at this juncture in a relationship he had run. This time he wasn't sure if he wanted to. Hell, he wasn't even sure he could. That made him angry and giddy at the same time. Having her involved with the Agency added another round of implications he would need to analyze. He just hoped he had not added a danger to her life that she was not prepared to deal with. Perhaps, some tutoring on how to stay alive in a dangerous world had just become urgent.

He was thoughtful rather than angry when he joined the others. Buster was naturally gregarious and soon Quint was drawn into a game of beach volleyball. The boys and Code were not going to be left out. Everyone was laughing as the kids and dog kept falling over one another. Quint glanced at Lila and grinned. When she winked back, he felt the sun shining into the dark places chasing out the negative thoughts that kept trying to lodge in his mind.

Lila edged next to him, "I should hit you with a boat paddle for keeping this place secret. I love it here."

"Hey, come anytime?"

"Watch it. I might take you up on that."

"Want to go to the house and audition?"

"Now?"

"I have no problem with it."

"Quint Cord, check with me later. Right now I am enjoying this."

"So much for being irresistible, huh?'

"So, pout!" Giving him a saucy grin she turned just in time to hit a volley back over the net.

Chapter 18

"Cousin, why have you avoided my phone calls? It is a problem for me to finance and assist someone who so callously disregards me. I do not care to have problems. It is my habit to eliminate them." Speaking in Arabic, Prince Fayed's voice was soft and the more menacing for being so.

Douglas Forsyth sputtered for a moment as he struggled to quell his fear. There was no mistaking the underlying threat to the words. He swallowed hard as his mind darted about to find the carefully rehearsed litany of reasons as to why he had not taken or returned calls from the Prince. It was as though memory had deserted him for a moment. At last he said into the continued silence on the line, "I would never deliberately avoid you. You must know how much I value you as a friend, as family, and as a fellow mujahid in the quest to destroy the kuffar President."

"Yes, we are warriors in the effort to destroy the infidel, but at the moment we seem to be warriors without any victory. Now, I believe you were going to explain why you have avoided me?"

"No, no, not avoid. I was in a highly confidential series of meetings with the President and could not get away to make a secure call to you. I asked my secretary to relay that to you and that I would call you as soon as it was possible. I must assume she failed to deliver my message."

"And I, I assume nothing. But, we will leave that for the moment as there are more important issues to address." The

Prince's voice tightened with anger. I had a casual visit from Ambassador Russell Chesson. He mentioned that the CIA has possession of a certain cell phone obtained from some unnamed source. It appears that this phone has calls from both you and me to the stupid dog that was to take care of the events in London. Due to an as yet unexplained tragedy, he is apparently dead. Dead before he could carry out his mission, I might add. I told you that there is no room for this kind of error. Just how do you plan to explain your acquaintance with this man? As for me, it was fairly simple. I said that he was a distant cousin that was calling me to ask for money after being disowned by his father for reckless behavior and that I had not seen him in years. You should expect a phone call from the CIA asking the same question. I can only hope you provide them with better answers than the ones you give me. Otherwise, you are rapidly becoming a risk that I cannot afford."

Before Forsyth could answer, the phone clicked off leaving only a buzzing in his ear. Cold sweat broke out across his brow and the pungent odor of fear exuded from his armpits. Following the fear came self-righteous anger. After all, he reasoned, he was not the one supplying the inept assholes needed to do the bombing and wet work. If that was the best the Prince had to offer, he should look to himself for the failures. Of course, Fayed's ego would never allow for that admission, so now Forsyth had to be the patsy. If he did not need the financial backing of Fayed, he would damn well ditch the son of a bitch. As it was, all he could do was figure a way out of the fiasco and try to get back in the Prince's good graces through some dramatic success. The question was always in the details: the 'what' and the 'how?'

Douglas Forsyth locked his office door. He then poured himself a healthy slug of the aged Scotch he favored and walked over to the window where he stood staring out at the city that would be the seat of his power when he succeeded in becoming the most powerful man in the world. He watched the relentless traffic below, the pedestrians scurrying along with hair and clothing whipped by the wind. The brewing storm matched his mood. He forced relaxation into his tense muscles and felt fear and anger draining away to be replaced by cold resolve. He ignored his secretary's insistent bussing and the shrill ring of his phone. To hell with them all, he needed time to think. Looking down into his glass, he saw that it was empty. Leaving the window he poured another before sitting back at his desk. Rocking back in his chair, he closed his eyes and slowly sipped. Little by little a plan was forming. Glancing at his watch he noted that it was past closing time for government agencies. Not long afterward he heard his outer office door close announcing the departure of his secretary. Chancing that the CIA Director's secretary had also left, he picked up his phone and dialed Gerald Williams' direct number hoping he would answer. He was in luck as the Director picked up on the third ring.

"Williams speaking."

"Gerald. Douglas Forsyth. I am glad I caught you, as I have been worrying about something. It probably has no significance, but then you never know."

"Shoot." Gerald was busy trying to sift through details that were slowly emerging relative to the terrorist plot in London and while calling Forsyth was on the his list of things to do, he was not yet ready to pursue that particular lead. The sooner he could get the man off the phone the happier he would be.

Forsyth forced a casual tone as he began, "You may recall I was in Saudi Arabia recently on a trade mission and it was written up in the local papers. I don't know if that is what triggered it, but I got a call after that from some guy introducing himself as a cousin of the Saudi royal family. He seemed to think I might be able to help him get back in their good graces by arranging a trade deal with some company he was working with. I don't remember the details and I didn't write anything down as I blew him off since I wanted to keep everything going through government channels. It probably has no significance but I thought you should know."

"That's interesting, but at the moment I wouldn't worry about it. If something comes up, I'll give you a call." Gerald smiled to himself at the coincidence. He never had put much stock in coincidences. "I was just leaving the office, so if there's nothing else..."

"No, not at all. Thank you for your time and please don't let me keep you."

Forsyth leaned back in his chair and congratulated himself on taking the initiative. He thought he had done well and hit just the right note. Hopefully that would keep the CIA from meddling in his business. Now all he needed to do was figure out something that would make the Prince happy enough to send more money. He knocked back a slug of scotch and then logged onto the Internet. During the next hour he tracked his first two targets and determined how best to take them out. Satisfied that he had the solution, he called a local number and then his wife. He might as well make amends with Rena since she could well be the new first lady in the not too distant future.

She answered on the second ring knowing he would be furious with her if it took any longer. "Hello, Douglas. Are you on the way home?"

"Darling, I haven't been very nice to you lately. I want to make it up to you. Get dressed in something pretty, pack an overnight bag and check into the Mayflower Hotel. I have already booked a suite. Lets have champagne and just celebrate."

"Celebrate? Has something happened?"

"Nothing. I just want to celebrate." His voice softened, "Do you have a problem with that?"

"Oh, no. I was just curious. When should I be there?"

"It's seven now, so no later than nine."

"That's fine. I'll be there."

Rena hung up the phone and looked across the kitchen counter at Teresa. "My husband wants me to meet him at the Mayflower for a *'romantic evening.'* I wonder what the bastard is up to."

"Don't go, Miss Rena. You know I don't trust that man. He's mean through and through."

"And just what do you think he would do to me if I don't do as he says? You know I have no choice. God help me."

"I do *pray He does* before that bastard kills you!"

"Rena, I need you to do me a favor. I'm going to give you a folder before I leave. Keep it safe for me and if something should ever happen to me, get it to the CIA. Don't keep it here. I'm afraid Douglas will find it."

Rena could feel the cook's eyes following her as she left the kitchen to dress and pack. It was so unlike Douglas to make a romantic overture. Rena wished she could take it as a hopeful sign that things would get better for her, but long years of disappointment would not allow her to draw that conclusion. Whatever he was up to she would learn soon enough. She could only pray for the best.

Going through the closet, she selected a low cut, clinging jersey knit that she had worn when they were dating. He had loved it on her then, but she had not worn it in years. Slipping it on, she noticed that it was not nearly as clinging as it had once been. She knew she had lost weight but was shocked when she looked in the mirror and could see how much. Rejecting it, she churned through the closet until she found one she had always considered both too tight and too revealing. At least it fit and with diminished curves the heavy silk fabric looked both elegant and sexy. She then did her hair in an upsweep and carefully applied her makeup. Modeling afterwards, she was pleased with the effect. If she was ever free of her husband, surely other men would find her attractive...that is, if she ever trusted a man again. Slipping on red Manolo Blanik pumps that complimented the white of the dress and her ruby and diamond jewelry, she hurriedly packed her overnight case. At the last minute she added a black silk nightgown and matching peignor. Grabbing a white mink shawl trimmed with black fox pompoms she hurried to the buzzer to signal the chauffer she was ready to leave.

Following the Mayflower bellboy to their room, she looked around at the attractive decor. She had long loved the hotel restaurant but had never stayed in the hotel before. The bellboy opened the door and led her in. She waited in the foyer while he took her bag to the bedroom, adjusted the thermostat, and returned, his palm up in the not-so-discrete manner of the less seasoned. Rena handed him a five-dollar bill and waited for him to leave. Walking into the living room of the suite, she saw that a fire was burning in the fireplace and a table draped with pristine linens and set for dinner awaited. On the chest beside the table a chilled bottle of champagne rested beside silver domed serving dishes. A soft melody was playing from somewhere in the background. She looked around in amazement before walking into the bedroom. There the bed was turned back and an arrangement of long stemmed roses decorated the bedside table. For whatever reason, her husband had gone to a great deal of trouble.

She had just walked back into the living room when she heard the foyer door open and Douglas walked in.

"So what do you think? Is this suitable for a celebration?"

"It's fabulous. But, what is the occasion?"

"Do we need one? By the way, you look especially lovely." He wagged his eyebrow suggestively, exuding the effortless charm that had first attracted her to him. "Let's begin with a glass of champagne, shall we?"

Rena felt hope beginning to spread through her followed by a happiness she had not felt in a very long time. Maybe, her marriage was going to be better in future if he would go to such lengths to please her. The dinner was everything she could have wished for. Afterwards, Douglas popped the cork on another bottle of Cristal champagne and beaconed her to join him at fireside. Rena rose from the table and sat beside him in front of the fire. They saluted one another with their champagne glasses as he poured a refill.

"Thank you, Douglas. This has been a wonderful evening. You have made me happy for the first time in a long time and so hopeful that our marriage will be better in future."

Well into the third bottle of champagne and becoming inebriated, he snarled in reply, "What makes you think it needs to be any better?"

"Please, I didn't mean anything by that.   Let's just be happy."

"I was, you bitch, until you make a comment like that."

Rena never saw the first punch coming. It knocked her so senseless she did not see the others either. Soon she lay insensate on the floor by the flickering fire. Douglas kicked her in the side before reeling into the bedroom where he crashed onto the bed fully dressed. He did not hear her soft groans in the night and would not have cared if he had. It was late in the morning when the sun shining through the crack in the drapes awakened him. Groggily moving to the shower he climbed in and relished the downpour of steaming water. After toweling off, he walked into the living room. His wife was lying on the floor where he had left her. He didn't know if she was dead, unconscious, or sleeping. The bruises that covering her face, and the parts of her exposed body, excited him. Wasting no time, he pulled up her dress and snatched off the scanty panties she wore. She was a beautiful woman and the more exciting in her helplessness before him. He had no compunction about taking her as she lay there. When he was finished he slapped her on the face.   She blinked at him in semi-awareness. Groaning, she tried to open her eyes more but her swollen lids allowed for a mere slit.

"You bitch.   You got exactly what you deserve. Unfortunately, I think you need to stay here for a few days. It wouldn't do for you to walk out of here looking like a train wreck. I'll arrange for room service to bring meals to the door and ring to let you know they are here. No need to let them in; you tell them to leave the tray by the door."

She blinked her eyes once in response before closing them against the sight of him gloating above her. She felt as though every bone in her body groaned in complaint when she dared to move even an inch. Lying there, she suspected at least one of her ribs was broken as it hurt every time she took all but the shallowest of breaths. On top of the physical agony was the deeper hurt of the final disappointment she would ever feel for her husband and their marriage. If nothing else, the previous night had taught her one thing. If she wanted to live and have any kind of life, she had to find a way to free herself of the monster she had married. Slow tears seeped from her eyes as she listened to Douglas dressing and preparing to leave. She heard him pick up the phone in the bedroom. Straining to hear, she lay quietly so if he looked into the living room he would not know that she was awake and listening.

"Prince Fayed, I took care of the matter of the phone taken from our guy in London by calling the CIA myself and expressing concern that this nobody had dared call me wanting favors."

She did not hear the Prince's response, but did hear her husband continue, "The Director totally bought it, so no more problems on that front. As for Paris and London, I have a plan for taking care of that immediately. I need you to have a team of assets in place near the center of both cities and expecting an email from Tony the Tiger. They need to be ready to move to the targets I give them in less than 20 minutes. They will need to work in at least two shifts so they are always ready to go. I'm not giving anymore advance lead time until I know whether or not the CIA is tracking and decoding my messages."

Douglas paused to listen before continuing, "No. That will be taken care of. All the teams need to do is following my instructions as to when and where. I think trucks loaded with explosives as well as suicide vests are the best solution. Have them in place by the day after tomorrow and I will take it from there. As soon as this is taken care of, I will begin on Washington."

She heard him laugh, before announcing to the empty bedroom, "Fayed, you just hung up on the future President of the United States."

Forcing herself to lie still and unresponsive, she heard him walk to her side and nudge the broken rib with his foot. She wanted to scream in pain but dared not react. Her only safety lay in allowing him to think she was unconscious.

He snarled, "You bitch, I've decided you just might not live long enough to be First Lady after all. I'm bored with you."

The door slammed behind him as he left. Rena prayed she would live long enough to get the new information to someone that could stop whatever evil he had planned. Even if she could not, the folder contained enough to incriminate him. If only she had listened to Teresa...

Chapter 19

"Christ!" Lila jumped up from her computer and dashed for the deck outside the bedroom where she scanned the beach for Quint. Jumping up and down, she wave frantically. Quint was so busy playing chase with the boys that he did not see her. Frustrated, she hurried down to the shore hollering as she ran.

Quint looked up once he realized she was calling him. Judging by the haste with which she was coming towards him and the note of panic in her voice, he knew something was wrong. Racing towards her, he grabbed her by the shoulders. "Hey, girl. What's up?"

"That Tony asshole just triggered something and I don't know how, where, when, or what. I just know it's going to be soon."

"Slow down and take it from the top."

"While I was rooting around looking for links that would lead us to TTT...that's my way of saying Tony the Tiger...this email popped up. All it said was "Go.""

"Wasn't it coded? How do you know that's what it said?"

"Because I hacked your email, lover boy. How else would I know? Your super secret spy bunch didn't think I needed to know. I don't play that way. If I'm putting my butt on the line, I want to know what I'm up against."

"I would ask for an apology but I suppose that would be pointless?"

"Damn straight! Now call *our* boss and tell him what's

going down."

"I wish I knew. I have a bad feeling that we won't have to wait long."

'I wish you were wrong, but I don't think so. While you're calling Gerald, I'll turn on the TV in the bedroom. No need to alarm the others."

Lila reached for Quint's hand as they walked into his bedroom and squeezed it not knowing if she was trying to reassure him or herself.   This was a serious world she discovered, far more so than she had believed when she accepted the Agency job. She flipped on the TV and tuned to the twenty-four hour cable news channel, Quint grabbed his cell phone from his shorts and dialed Gerald's private number.

Gerald had just arrived at his office when he answered, "Yeah, what's up?"

"Nothing good I'm afraid. Lila just intercepted a message from Tony the Tiger saying "go." And that's all it said. We don't know what he just triggered, but I think it will be soon. We've got the TV on to see what's breaking."

Gerald swore under his breath, "Hold on. I'm turning to the news channel. As of now nothing has come through here from intelligence so I am as in the dark as you are.

They both said "shit" at the same time as they watched their screens shift to dual live feeds from both London and Paris. Flashing blue lights and the wail of sirens underscored some tragic event had occurred simultaneously in both cities.

"What were the targets do you think?" Quint asked.

"At this point your guess is as good as mine."   Gerald paused, "Hey, I've got to go. The White House is calling and I suspect I have to deal with one damned angry President, as I gave him no heads-up that something might be in the works.

"Yeah, but we both know these fuckers don't work that way. We are the ones that announce everything to the world." Quint was angry and he could sense that Gerald was as well. The trouble was until they could nail the Tiger they were fumbling in the dark trying to grab hold of something on which to hang a case.

"Later."

Quint nodded even though Gerald could not see him. "Sure, take that call from the President. I will keep you posted if we get anything."

Gerald clicked the line where the President's secretary was waiting for him to pick up. "Gerald Williams here."

"Please hold the line, Mr. Director." In less than two seconds, the President was on the other end.

President Clayton Northrup wasted no time with subtleties, "What in the hell is going on? I just got off the phone with Prime Minister Grantham asking me about terrorist ties to the US in this latest London bombing. Immediately after that, I get a call from France asking the same thing. In case you haven't heard, the rising star in the Tory party along with several other members of Parliament were bombed in a London restaurant a few minutes ago. They are all dead. Thirty other diners were either killed or wounded. In Paris, the son-of-a-bitches murdered the President and killed five in his security detail and wounded the sixth who managed to kill them. Unfortunately for us, the terrorists were all killed, both in London and Paris. I say unfortunately because they all were carrying US passports. I need something fast to point the finger in another direction so we don't have our two oldest allies out for our asses."

"I'll get with MI6 and have the passport photos faxed over. France will do the same, I'm sure. We'll run them through the system and see what we come up with. It is atypical for these savages to have any identification on them. There is a good chance the passports are fakes as I think the mastermind is using Arab talent for their wet work. I'm afraid that will not be the end of it though. There well may be a US connection."

"Dammit, I didn't need to hear that. This goes from bad to worse. What else have you got?"

"Sir, I cannot prove it, but there is a good chance someone high up here in Washington is pulling the strings with the help of a Saudi Prince."

"Fuck! Throw everything we've got at it. Get back to me as soon as you have anything I can use to deflect blame from our government. And find that damned traitor." He slammed the phone down without waiting for Gerald to respond.

*****

At that moment, several miles away the elated Saudi Prince had just dialed Forsyth's office. This time the Speaker felt no trepidation in taking the call. He could not prevent the gloating note in his voice when he answered. "Praise be to Allah! We did it, Fayed. We damned well did it. And as the American's say, the fat is in the fire. Now to take care of this side of the pond and we are on the way to achieving all of our goals."

"I am pleased that my investment is finally paying off. You will received the next payment as promised. However, there are several loose ends that need tying up before we proceed in Washington. We cannot afford any mistakes from here on out. It is critical we eliminate any potential problems. The doctor husband of that secretary and that code breaker both need to disappear...permanently."

"I don't think the husband knows anything and the code breaker doesn't seem to have broken my code. If we take them out, the CIA director is going to be pretty damned mad and looking even more closely into his secretary's death. As for Cord, there is always going to be another code breaker somewhere."

The Prince forced himself to swallow the words 'I don't pay you to think.' Instead he snarled, "Take them out. Use Jamal and the other guy that killed that secretary woman. Try to make it look like a car accident or something if you're worried, but if that cannot be, just do it."

"I'll see what I can do, but it won't be so easy as the CIA has them safely tucked away somewhere. It is going to take time to set up some kind of surveillance to find them. The best bet is a good hacker into the email chains."

"Do you have someone?"

"Maybe, but I will have to be beyond discreet and I don't know how good he is." The last thing he wanted to do was involve his hacker in murders. If the man were caught he could well squeal to save his own hide. Forsyth did not need the added risk. "It would be better if you could put someone on it from there. We cannot afford any slip-ups when we're so close to our goal."

"Absolutely not. I provide the jhadists and the money. It's up to you to do the rest. Of course, if you cannot handle it....?" The Prince did not wait for a reply.

Forsyth sat at his desk for long moments listening to the buzz from the disconnected line. He wondered if it were all worth it. When he began his road to power he had not considered the costs and consequences, or the substantial risks to his own life. Another immediate problem was his wife. He had not intended to beat her that badly. He regretted the complication if not the action. She got what she had coming to her was the way he figured it. But, he was going to have to figure out what to do about the bitch until her face healed enough she could go home. He wasn't too worried about the cook, however it wouldn't hurt to call and tell her they would be away for a couple of days more and not to plan meals. He would let Teresa think that they were enjoying a romantic holiday at the luxury hotel. The damned room was costing him enough he might as well stay there, too.

Before he left the office he placed a call to a private detective who for enough money would ask no questions. Hopefully Sam Reynolds would track down Marlowe's husband and the CIA code breaker, Quinton Cord. He did not agree with the Prince but he dared not defy him. In his opinion it was far more risky to go after them than it was to let things ride until they had reason to worry. Shutting down his computer, he stuffed several files into his brief case and after a parting word to his secretary, left for the hotel.

The concierge smiled at him as he entered the lobby. Without breaking stride Forsyth nodded his head in acknowledgement of the greeting as he headed for the elevator. He pushed the button for the penthouse suite and fidgeted with impatience as he ascended. Walking down the luxuriously carpeted hallway, he arrived at the suite's door and inserted the magnetic card. He walked into the suite to find his wife lying on the floor where he had left her, a pool of vomit under her head. Muttering a curse, he walked over and bent down to check her pulse. He wouldn't put it past the bitch to die on him before he could figure out how to deal with her. Although her pulse was rapid and faint, and her skin cyanotic, she was at least alive. Sighing with relief, he picked her up and carried her to the bed. She moaned in pain as he lay her down. Slowly her eyes blinked open. He watched as they registered recognition, then fear.

"I'm going to get a washcloth and clean you up. You stink like a pig in shit."

He returned to find that she had not moved. Slowly he wiped her face and cleansed the residue from her hair. That done he studied her carefully. Her breathing had a crackling noise that suggested a lung was punctured. That left him two options. He could take her to the hospital and deal with a lot of uncomfortable questions and the possibility of arrest for battery and spousal abuse, or he could arrange for her to disappear. It was a no-brainer as far as he was concerned. Fumbling in his pocket, he dialed the number for Jamal Kalil.

"I have another job for you. I need you to get hold of a uniform for the Mayflower Hotel staff and a large laundry bag. I don't care how you do it as long as no one catches you. When you have them, dress in the uniform, hide the bag under your jacket, and come to the penthouse. Tell the other guy to wait in the car until you return with the package."

"What kind of package?"

"What the fuck do you care? For the money you get paid, I don't need to answer questions. Now get your ass here."

As Rena listened to husband there was no question in her mind that he planned to kill her. A small quiet voice in her head wanted her to fight for her life, but she had no energy left and no desire to go on living in the hell Douglas had created for her.

She whispered, "You won't get away with it *Tony the Tiger*. I know who you are and what you are up to. I've known for a long time."

"Who gives a shit? Dead women don't talk." Forsyth sneered down at her, "That's your damned trouble. You never have known when to shut up. If you had, things might have been a lot different between us."

He walked into to the living room of the suite and dialed room service where he ordered a meal for two and a bottle of champagne. He might as well enjoy his coming bachelorhood with a celebration, especially considering what he was paying for the damned suites. As he hung up, he noticed the vomit on the carpet and swore. He would have to clean that up and spray some of Rena's perfume around to mask the odor. When that was accomplished, he walked to the bedroom closet and snatched down the sexy peignoir to drape over the sofa in the living room. He planned to set the stage so afterwards were the steward that delivered the room service cart questioned, he could say that the Representative and his wife appeared to be in the middle of a romantic evening. To increase the ambiance he turned on soft music. Just before room service buzzed the door, he turned on the shower in the bath.

Forsyth opened the door with a huge smile on his face, "Wonderful, you are right on time. My wife is about finished with her shower, so this will give me time to open the champagne."

"I am happy to do that for you, sir."

"No, no. This is fine. I can take it from here. We're celebrating." He winked knowingly at the Steward.

The steward palmed the generous tip, thanked Forsyth and left. Wasting no time, he popped the cork on the champagne and poured himself a glass. He looked at it for a moment before getting another idea. Going to the well-stocked bar, he found a bottle of bourbon that he took to the bedroom and dribbled into his wife's hair and on her gown. Satisfied with the aroma arising from his seemingly unconscious wife, he returned to the cart in the living room, served two plates and tucked into his with gusto. Rena's he would leave with the food merely stirred around a bit. Sated he wiped his mouth with his napkin. Picking up her fork and napkin he returned to the bedroom to wrap her fingers around the fork and blot her mouth with the napkin. She stirred restlessly but did not awaken. He then dropped them carelessly on the cart by her plate. Noticing her empty champagne glass, he poured in a splash and returned to the bedroom to put it to her mouth to pick up her lip print and then he pressed it into her hand. That done he walked back to the bar and poured bourbon into the stem. He then carried it back to the bedside table. He had done all he knew to do. Now he had only to wait for Jamal.

Chapter 20

Teresa had worried since the moment Rena left the house to go meet her husband. She had heard nothing from her since. The cook was sitting at the kitchen table nibbling at her fingernail while a cup of coffee grew cold. She had hidden the folder Rena had given her at her sister's house. It nagged at her. If something happened to Rena, did she dare turn it over to the government? Whom should she give it to and what if Douglas Forsyth found out what she had done? Would she ever be safe again? She was so lost in thought that she did not at first hear the ringing phone. When it finally registered, she jumped up from the table to grab it from the wall by the refrigerator.

"Teresa," Forsyth began without waiting for her to say hello, "We have decided to stay another night. Tomorrow night I want you to have a special dinner waiting for us. We should get there around seven. Make sure you cook all of the dishes you know my wife loves and chill a nice bottle or two of champagne."

"Yes, sir. I'll do that. Do you think I could speak to Miss Rena, sir?"

"She's in the shower. She told me to tell you hello and that she is looking forward to coming home."

"Yes, sir. I'll see y'all tomorrow night." Teresa eased the phone back in the cradle, but left her hand resting on it. She did not trust the man, never had, and something in his voice made the hairs on her neck stand on end. At bedtime she said a long prayer for Rena's safety, but sleep proved elusive.

Getting up the next morning, she tried to shake off her unease while she ran errands to buy fresh flowers and the items she would need to make dinner. Once she was working in her kitchen, the demands of the dishes she was preparing took her mind off anything else.

Douglas Forsyth was uneasy, too. Telling Jamal and his cohort, Mohammed, to rape Rena before killing her created too much of a connection to the murder of Marlowe Hollings. Unfortunately he could not think of a better plan at the spur of the moment. It wouldn't be long before a connection was made if they were able to find DNA. Hopefully they would burn her body well enough that nothing would be left to point to the connection. That left disposal of the damned code breaker and Dr. Hollings. He did not dare tell the Prince that he had been forced to kill his wife as well.

He sat at his desk twirling his pen while he waited for the hours to tick by. His private detective was on the trail of Cord and Hollins thanks to an insider at the Agency with a loose mouth and looser morals. He should know where they were by the end of the day. Once his assets took them out, he would see to it that the hit men were next. He could not afford for any loose ends to lead back to him. While he waited for the detective to call, he toyed with various scenarios to explain why his wife was not with him when he arrived home that night.

He would have been much happier on the drive to his house as he sat fuming at not receiving the expected call if he had known that Gerald Williams had just decided that the doctor and Quint were no longer in danger.

*****

Once the call came to the safe house, the doctor wasted no

time in returning to his office where his partner, Chris Wafford, was becoming increasingly frustrated by Hollins' continued absence. At the end of the day he delayed returning to his house, as he was not ready to face the emptiness in the rooms and in his heart. He suspected he would continue to work late and it would be a long time before he could do more than sleep in their bed.

After his call to the safe house, Gerald called Quint and then his wife. Jill was to pack up and have Buster drive her and the boys back to Washington where a newly secured house awaited them. Once they left the following morning and the extra security cleared out, Quint was going to be alone at the beach house, as Lila had already returned to Raleigh and her job at the university. Despite Gerald's warning that he was going to want him in Washington shortly, Quint thought of going back to Raleigh and his house there, but he decided to stay on a few days after everyone left. He told Gerald he loved his time walking along the shore to clear his mind and to focus on any messages that he might be able to intercept. Both he and Gerald were praying that any future messages would be in the same code and would give them enough lead-time to thwart any future attack. The attacks in London and Paris were still creating diplomatic and political repercussions for the President. Also, with enough time Lila hopefully would be able to track the message to its origin so they could nail whoever was behind it.

*****

Forsyth leaned back in his seat and finished the last of his scotch as the chauffeur turned into the gated entry to his home. He always felt a surge of pride when he rounded the bend and the imposing Georgian mansion loomed into view. Tonight was no different. He smiled to himself as he anticipated finding a new woman. If it were not a political impediment he would take a Muslim one, as they knew how to behave better than these American infidels. Unfortunately he must choose not only a wife, but also one suited to the future status of First Lady. Despite many advances in liberal quarters he did not think the country was ready for a Muslim First Lady. He could not afford any fingers digging into his own Muslim past.

Teresa met him at the rear vestibule door, a huge smile of welcome on her face. Forsyth handed her his wife's overnight bag and returned the smile, "It's good to be home. We're looking forward to one of your dinners."

Looking around him to find Rena, her face fell. She could not stop her voice trembling when she asked, "I thought Miss Rena was coming home with you?"

"Oh, you mean she isn't here yet? She should have been. She said she was going to the salon for a hair appointment but I assumed she would have been here by now. If she doesn't show up in the next few minutes, I'll call and see what's keeping her."

"Would you like a drink while you wait? I have some hors d'oeuvres, too."

"That's fine. Why don't you bring it into the den? No point in letting those hors d'oeuvres get stale, now is there?" He gave her a wink, "You know how I love them."

"Yes, sir. I'll bring them right in."

He walked down the hall whistling. She shook her head in wonder. Maybe their little holiday had done some good after all.

Forsyth walked into his den and flicked on the television and his laptop computer. He the settled back in his wing back chair, kicked off his shoes, and pulled the ottoman over to prop his feet. It felt good to be home. He could hear Teresa setting the table in the dining room. When she appeared in the doorway to the den, he motioned to the coffee table. "You can put the tray there. I'll open the champagne myself."

"Yes, sir."

He watched her while she arranged the tray. He could tell she wanted to ask him something.

Working her hands in her apron like she was trying to wring it, she looked up and met his watchful eyes, "I was just wondering if you had called Miss Rena to see if she is on the way home?"

"It slipped my mind. I'll call now."

In the distance, Teresa heard the faint distinctive tone of Rena's cell phone. She left the doorway and walked to the foot of the stairs where the overnight bag leaned against the lowest riser. The ringing was coming from within. She was trembling as she walked back to the den where Forsyth sat with his phone at his ear. Glancing her way, he commented, "She doesn't seem to be answering."

"She doesn't have her cell phone, sir. It's in her overnight bag."

"Damn. She must have forgotten it."

Teresa struggled to keep her voice level, "I suppose so. Do you want me to put dinner back to stay warm?"

"Well, since I don't know when she will be home, I might as well go ahead and eat. Just make a plate for her and put it aside."

"Yes, sir. Will you be wanting me to bring the second bottle of champagne you asked for, too?"

Forsyth grinned, "Why not.

Teresa finished serving him then sat at the kitchen counter to eat her own dinner. Even though it was one of her favorite meals worry for Rena kept her from enjoying it. After only a few bites, she gave up and sat brooding. When Forsyth rang the bell signaling that he was finished with the meal, she picked up the serving tray and walked through the butler's pantry to the dining room. Her mind was made up.

"Mr. Forsyth, sir, I am mighty worried about Miss Rena. This just ain't like her. I was wondering if maybe we should call the police?"

"It is too soon to alarm ourselves. Besides in the case of missing adults, they aren't going to do anything for twenty-four hours anyway. I feel sure she will show up soon although I cannot imagine what is keeping her. I know she was looking forward to coming home tonight." Forsyth shook his head as though puzzled. A slight tick in his right eye betrayed his seeming calm. "Try not to worry. If she doesn't come soon I will make some discreet inquiries. In my position, this is highly sensitive. I hope you appreciate that?"

Teresa had her hands clenched behind her back to keep him from seeing her shaking, "Yes, sir. I know you are an important man in the government. Do you think somebody would snatch her to get at you? I know you've had some threats."

"I'm trying not to think the worst and I suggest you do the same." Douglas arose from his chair signaling an end to the conversation. "I'll be upstairs if you need anything else."

Teresa began putting the dishes on the tray without

responding. Deep in her gut she knew something was wrong. For one thing, it had been months since he had allowed his wife the freedom to go anywhere without the chauffer tagging along like a watchdog. Why would he have left her to go alone to a salon and take taxis? Maybe they had reached some kind of turning point in their marriage for the better, but she didn't believe it for a minute. Taking a deep breath to steady herself she carried the loaded tray to the kitchen. The packet of papers Rena had given her weighed on her mind. Should she slip them to someone in the government? To whom could she give them so that the trail would not lead back to her? With his power and connections, would Forsyth not soon know? If he would not hesitate to do something to his own wife, of what worth was a cook's life? *Please, God,* she prayed, *just let Miss Rena walk back though that door one more time.* If she did, Teresa swore she would get her away from this house if it were the last thing she ever did.

As she washed the champagne stem, she heard Forsyth leave his den. She guessed he was going to bed. It amazed her that the man exhibited such calm with his wife missing. As she was returning the glass to the cabinet, she heard his voice behind her. Startled, she dropped the glass and watched it shatter on the granite countertop. She turned to face him.

"Don't worry about that. It can be replaced," Forsyth said as he motioned towards the shards with his hand. "Rena mentioned she had left some papers here that she wanted me to have. Do you know anything about them?"

Teresa sucked in her breath and held it for a beat. Forcing herself to meet his eyes and keeping her voice even, she replied, "No, sir. I don't know anything about any papers."

"That's fine. Don't worry about it. I'm sure she will give them to me when she gets home."

"You going to bed, Mr. Forsyth?"

"I might as well. It appears my wife is going to be late."

"Yes, sir. It does seem that way."

She did not know if he heard her or not as she was talking to his back as he hurried from the kitchen. She would bet that he was going to look for those papers. What puzzled her was how he knew about them or was he just guessing?

Chapter 21

Robbie Hollins sat at his desk rubbing his jaw. His partner and the rest of the staff had been gone for over an hour. He was bone tired but it felt good to be back at work. The worst time was the end of the day when he dreaded going home to his empty house. His patients were happy to have him back and a few had even brought flowers for the office or home baked goodies to cheer him up. One or two were recent divorcees on the prowl for a conquest. He chortled to himself as he recalled their inventive maladies. None of them could begin to hold a candle to Marlowe. Thinking of his wife reminded him he had slept little the last few nights. Several times in his sleep he had reached for her to pull her against him in the spoon position he favored. Each time he had awakened to the realization that he would never hold her again, never know the child she carried with her into death. The familiar bed they had shared was now cold and lonely. Perhaps he would redecorate and get everything new. He would think about that later as he was too tired to deal with it at the moment. He resolved to have a nice dinner at one of their favorite restaurants and then go home to a good bottle of wine. Maybe it would relax him enough to sleep.

Shaking his head, he rose from the desk and slipped on his jacket. The unfamiliar bulk of a loaded pistol reminded him of the warning his CIA babysitters had given him. Just because they did not believe he was any longer in danger did not mean that it was a guarantee. When they asked him if he could shoot, he remembered smiling as he recalled his record on his college

ROTC sharp-shooting team. Reaching over he turned off the computer on his desk, pushed his chair into place and glanced around the office.

Movement on the security-monitoring screen caught his eye. Someone had jimmied the poorly secured front office door that he had been meaning to have reworked and not gotten around to it. As he watched, two swarthy men with drawn weapons did a visual search of the reception area. Swallowing the momentary panic, he took a deep breath. All of the rage and pain of the previous night focused his resolve on retribution. A vessel in his forehead throbbed as he planned what he would do. From the description of the man that had forced his wife into their car, the lead one seemed to be a match. He fully intended to kill him and the other one as well. While it would not bring back his wife, at least he would rest easier knowing they could never again do to another woman what they did to her.

He slipped his shoes from his feet and tiptoed to stand behind his office door. A coat rack stood next to him with his white physician's coat hanging on it. The coat and rack gave him some cover and if the invaders slammed the door back it would hit the rack and not him. The click of the pistol as he armed it sounded loud in the silent office and he prayed they had not heard it through the closed door. A cold adrenalin triggered sweat trickled down his armpits, sending up a faint odor of fear. He hoped they came before his scent could betray him. Seconds felt like hours as he waited for them to open the door. There was no doubt in his mind that they intended to kill him. He heard muted footsteps as they crept down the tiled hall. It was apparent they intended to surprise and take him out before he could react.

He trained his gun on the door at chest height and tensed his finger on the trigger. The door slammed back and for a split second he frozen before squeezing off a round at the first man through. The man spiraled to the floor without so much as a whimper. Ducking lower, Robbie fired again and again scored a hit. He hadn't killed this one. The man had dropped his weapon and was writhing in pain. Walking up to him, Robbie kicked the gunman's weapon across the office and trained his own on him. He then edged over to the first man and slowly squatted to check for pulse. There was nothing.

A third man suddenly appeared in the door. Hollins swung his gun at him and was ready to squeeze off a shot when the man ducked out of sight and hollered. "For the love of God, don't shoot. I'm with the CIA. You can call the director, Gerald Williams if you need to verify."

"So, who the hell are you and what are you doing here?"

"I'm Quint Cord, Dr. Hollins. I met your late wife and spoke to her on the phone as well. I have been sequestered just like you until a few days ago. I just wanted to stop by and express my sympathies now that I am back in Washington. I was driving by and saw your light on and pulled in on the spur of the moment. I heard the shots when I came in and thought you might need help more than sympathy."

"Slide your weapon past that door and put your hands in the air."

Quint did as he was instructed.

When the doctor saw the weapon slide past the doorway, he called, "Alright, fish out your CIA-ID and step out with your hands up so I can see both you and the badge."

Quint stepped into the door of the office and carefully

handed over his badge. While Hollins glanced at his badge, he stared at the floor in amazement, "Well, Doc, it looks like you had some unwelcome guests. If they are your patients, I sure wouldn't want you doctoring on me."

Hollins was in no mood for humor, "You think you are a real smart ass. Why don't you make yourself useful and call Director Williams and tell him we need some help over here."

The CIA number was on fast dial. It only rang once before it was picked up.

Quint drawled, "Guess things aren't as safe for me and the doctor as you thought. He just shot some intruders. One is dead in his office floor. Another one appears to have a thigh wound that struck one of the femoral arteries. He'll be dead in minutes, I suspect."

Williams' voice was tightly controlled when he replied, "I assume you must be with him. Hand the phone to Dr. Hollins, Quint."

Hollins took Quint's phone and responded, "Yeah, it's me."

"Can you keep him alive? It might be helpful if we could question him and find out who he's working for."

"I'd rather he was dead like the other one, but I take your point. Just get someone to haul ass over here and help us with this mess."

"Agent Burke is rolling as I speak. Do what you can for the bastard." He paused, "You guys keep an eye out for trouble. There probably aren't any more but it pays to be careful."

"I'll do my best. Now let me see what I can do to save this fucking asshole."

While Hollins applied a tourniquet to the injured man's thigh, Quint knelt beside the dead man and began a methodical search of his pockets. He fished out keys and inhaler from his left pocket. "Guess he won't be troubled by asthma anymore."

The doctor glanced over and shook his head without commenting.

"Hey, don't make that asshole too comfortable, Doc. I think he should suffer a little just for the hell of it."

"If it was up to me, I would practice some surgical techniques on him without benefit of anesthesia. However, Mr. Williams said to keep him alive for questioning."

Quint grinned and continued searching while the doctor washed up and dug in his cabinet for the sterile instruments needed to clamp off the artery and extract the bullet. In the body's right pocket Quint found a cell phone, chewing gum, and a spring-loaded knife, in the other was a wallet. He flipped it open and found no ID, as he expected with professional killers. Next he moved beside the doctor and proceeded to search the other man's pockets. He carried no ID, no wallet, nothing in the pocket except lint. He scraped that out just in case it might contain some microscopic bit that could be of use.

He picked up the dead man's cell phone wishing he could access the database. He almost dropped it when it rang unexpectedly. Noting a DC exchange number, he shoved it at the barely conscious man and growled, "In English, 'say everything is taken care of at the doctor's.' You say another damned word and you're going to be praying for me to kill you fast. Do you understand me?"

The man nodded and answered repeating Quint's words. The minute he had finished, Quint ended the call and scribbled the caller's number on the doctor's prescription pad. Turning back to the injured man, he said, "What's your name?"

The man looked at him with contempt and spat. Quint did not even bother to wipe the glob from his sleeve before he grabbed him. Glaring at the man, Quint squeezed hard on his wound. "You want to live asshole, you will answer my question now."

"Mohammed." The man groaned as Quint continued squeezing.

"Don't make it so hard, Mohammed. What's the rest of your fucking name?"

"Kalil."

Continuing the painful pressure on Mohammed's wound, Quint growled, "What is the name of your dead buddy?"

"Jamal."

"I'm getting real tired of your shit." Mohammed screamed as Quint squeezed harder.

"Hussein. Jamil Hussein."

"Who just called you guys?"

"I don't know, honest"

Again Quint gripped the wound, Mohammed pleaded, "Please, he never told us his name. I'm not lying."

"Now listen real good, asshole: we are going to nail whoever the fucker is that hired you. I've got a personal grudge to settle with him and you, too. If you know what's smart you'll play real nice. Fun and games are over for you."

His voice grim, Hollins remarked, "I already had a grudge, as well. Now I have another one since killing my wife wasn't enough. Now they are trying to take me out, too."

"Yeah, I know." Quit touched Hollins on the arm, "You did good, Doc. While you are working on Mohammed, I'm going to go up front and keep an eye out."

"Holler if you need any help. I'm a pretty good shot."

Quint cocked an eyebrow as he glanced at the two men and said, "Damned straight."

Quint settled into the receptionist desk which gave him a clear view of the door and would provide cover if he needed it. He had not been there long when the shadow of a man, backlit by a corridor light, showed through the translucent glass. Sliding down to the floor with the gun and his eyes trained on the man he waited for the door to open. He lowered his gun and sighed with relief when he recognized Agent Burke. Another two men he had not met entered with Burke.

Charles Burke smiled in recognition, "Well, Mr. Code-Breaker, what are you doing in our neck of the woods?"

"The Director ordered my ass to Washington this morning or I'd still be sitting on the beach. Who are your buddies?"

Pointing to a man built like a defensive back, Burke grinned. Quint Cord, this is Agent Wallace Denton, otherwise known as 'Tiny' for some reason."

Denton laughed good-naturedly and stuck out his hand. "Fuck you, Burke. It's good to finally meet you, Quint. I've heard nothing but good things."

"Thanks, you too."

"The other joker is Agent James Abrams."

"Nice to meet you, James." Quint shook the pro-offered hand before gesturing towards the back, "Come on. The doctor had some callers earlier. Names are Jamal Hussein and Mohammed Kalil. He killed Jamal and wounded the other. Doc's working on him now."

"Not to worry. We're going to tidy things up and see what we can find."

"The injured guy had nothing in his pockets. I searched the dead one and put his stuff on the floor beside him. His phone rang and I had Mohammed answer it and say everything's cool. I cut him off before he could say anything else. The number of the caller is on a piece of paper by the phone. Hopefully it will lead us to whoever is pulling their strings."

Burke turned to Abrams, directing him to collect the guns. Abrams pulled on the gloves he extracted from his pocket and then fumbled for several plastic bags. He picked up the guns and dropped them in separate bags. Denton followed the same procedure as he gathered the items by Jamal's body. Abrams retrieved a body bag from the brief case slung over his shoulder. Between them, the agents rolled the body into the bag and zipped it up. Hefting it on his shoulder, Denton said, "I'll be back as soon as I dump this dead garbage in the van."

Burke nodded, and turned to Hollins, "Doctor, it's a lucky break for us you have a polished marble floor as it will make clean up a lot easier. Where do you keep cleaning supplies? When we finish this office is going to look like nothing ever happened. I don't want your staff talking when they arrive in the morning. We're going to keep this quiet until the Director decides how he wants to handle it. When you get this sack of shit stable, we're going to put him in the van with his buddy."

"You don't want to take him to the hospital? He's lost enough blood he needs a transfusion. Even if he gets one soon, he could still die of hypovolemic shock due to exsanguination."

"Fuck! Can't he live without one?"

"Maybe, but he won't recover as fast if he makes it."

"I'm not real worried about his long-term prospects, but I'll check with the Director." The agents didn't appear to be concerned about making things any easier on the wounded Arab, nor were they in any hurry to call the director. At the moment, they were far more intent on cleaning up the mess. When the office looked normal, they put all of the soiled items in a garbage bag to take with them.

Just as they stuffed the last trash into the bag, Quint's phone rang. Glancing at the screen, he turned to Burke and said, "It's Director Williams. I'll ask him what he wants us to do with that fucker."

Williams wasted no time, "Quint, I need you to get over here ASAP. Lila just intercepted another message. She says the code looks the same but it no longer makes any sense. I need you to figure out what's up."

"I'm on my way. Before you ring off, Agent Burke wants to know if you want the injured perp taken to the hospital or to Buster's hide-away for a little question and answer session?"

"Will he live if he doesn't go to the hospital? We can't afford for him to die before we get answers and we may need him for a witness against whoever hired him."

"Doctor says he needs a transfusion, but he might make it without one."

"Ask the doctor to go with Burke to Buster's and to take whatever medical stuff he might need with him. I'll send someone with a saline solution and blood plasma as soon as we can get his blood type. Tell Hollins to get a sample of blood from the wounded man and bring it with you along with the cell phone when you come. The rest of the evidence can wait. I'll pick it up when I get to Buster's. How long do you think it will be before they can leave?"

"Ten minutes max."

"Right. I'll call Buster and warn him to expect company. I should be there no more than a couple of hours or so after they arrive."

"I'm coming with you." Quint knew he was out of line when he said it. He did not intend to be left out of the questioning session. All he could do was hope the Director would not object. When the Hendersons were killed it became personal.

Quint held his breath when Williams did not immediately respond. Finally he said, "You can go with me on one condition. I want that damned code cracked and you are not leaving my office until you have. If it is cracked by the time I leave, fine."

"Then I guess I had better not waste any time getting there." Quint slid his phone in his pocket and sighed.

Turning to the other men in the office, he said, "Doc you need to go with the agents. Take any kind of medical equipment, drugs, etc. with you. The Director is going to send blood and saline solution as soon as we get Mohammed's blood type."

"Fine with me. I want in on this, too."

Quint then relayed Gerald Williams message to the agents. All three agents nodded their heads. Burke handed him the plastic bag containing the gun and the phone number. The doctor had already collected a small vial of blood that he gave to Quint. Burke and Denton picked up Mohammed and headed to the black van waiting at the office building entrance. Abrams followed with the bag of bloody trash.

Hollins turned to Quint and said, "I have everything I will need. I just have to lock the door behind me and set the alarm."

Quint's mouth quirked up at one corner before he said, "Seems a bit like shutting the barn door, etc. At any rate, I'm out of here. Hopefully I'll see you later tonight."

Hollins reach out to shake Quint's hand, "I'm glad you showed up when you did."

"Yeah, I am, too."

When Quint reached his blue Toyota rental car, the black van's engine was idling as the agents waited for the doctor to exit the building. Squealing tires, Quint headed for the Interstate. In the rear view mirror he could see Hollins jumping in the van before it, too, left with tires squealing.

Chapter 22

Quint was sitting at a laptop in the Director's office. He had been there only thirty minutes when he looked up and addressed Gerald Williams. "I've got it! These stupid jerks are not real inventive. All the guy did was reverse the counting order of the letters. In this one he started at the bottom and counted up rather than from top down. Then he started from the right and counted left rather than vice versa."

"Skip the details and just tell me what it says," Gerald demanded.

"It says, and I quote: 'As you ordered, the doctor is taken care of. Cord is in the process of being eliminated. Ready to proceed to President and Vice President. Will advise."

"Do you know who it's from and to whom it was sent?"

"Lila's working on that angle. She's the whiz at that kind of thing, not me. Now, do I get to go with you to Buster's?"

"Sure. And Quint, thanks. I appreciate all you have done and I'll make sure the President and the Vice President's security teams know they are targets."

"No Problem."

Gerald and Quint looked up as an agent entered the office carrying a medical package. "Sir, this is the blood and saline solution you ordered. We're working on DNA samples from the two perps and should have that soon."

"The sooner the better. When you have them, see if they match with the DNA from the sperm samples we took from the Hollins woman." Gerald nodded in dismissal.

"Looks like we are ready to go," he indicated the private exit door to Quint.

Both men stood. Quint grabbed the medical bag and his laptop as the director informed his secretary he was leaving. Since it was now well after ten, she was going to be one happy lady to go home and get some sleep. Just as they reached the exit door, the private line on his desk began to ring. For a moment Gerald was tempted to ignore it.

"Crap. I'd better get it," he muttered. Picking up the phone, he said, "Director Williams speaking."

"Director, I'm so glad I caught you. This is Douglas Forsyth. My wife is missing and I'm really worried. I've had some threats lately. It looks like I shouldn't have shrugged them off."

"How long has she been missing?"

"She was supposed to get her hair done this afternoon and then be home by seven or so. She never showed up. That's just not like Rena."

"Email me the name of the salon. I'll have someone check them out first thing in the morning if she doesn't show up. Since she is an adult, it will be at least twenty-four hours before the police will do anything."

"I know, I know! That's why I called you," Forsyth said, forcing his voice to sound slightly hysterical. "I don't know the name of the salon or I would have called it. You do know there have been threats against me? Maybe, they decided to go after my wife instead."

"Calm down. It's probably nothing, but if she still is not back by morning give me a call."

"Thank you. I'm sorry to bother you so late. I'll let you know one way or another in the morning."

"Fine. Now, try to get some sleep and not worry. It's probably nothing." Gerald wasn't so sure, but he allowed no indication of his uncertainty to creep into his voice. He had met Forsyth's wife on several occasions and if there was ever an unhappy woman, she filled the bill. She was beautiful and poised every time he had seen her, but when her husband looked at her she seemed to panic like a rabbit looking for a bolt hole.

He let his hand rest on his phone after he hung up. "Damn, that was curious."

Quint squinted in inquiry.

"Douglas Forsyth says his wife has gone missing. It's early yet to make that assumption. We'll see what the morning brings."

"Yeah, things get curiouser and curiouser. I'd just like to know how these guys knew the Doc was back at work and I'm in Washington?"

"Either they were watching his office, or someone is a leak at the agency. As for you, I'm not sure. I don't think they know you were at your beach house. Did you go by the Raleigh house before you flew here?"

"Shit. They must have someone watching it. Yeah, I went by to pick up some clean clothes and check on things there. I took Code to a kennel since I couldn't bring him with me." He didn't see the need to add that he had swung by Lila's for a little bedtime sport.

"My boys are going to be pissed with you. You know they would have kept him."

Gerald smiled when he thought about it. His brow wrinkled with worry as his smile faded. "Let's hope it was simple surveillance on you two and not a leak. Since Marlowe's death, I had everyone in the agency re-background checked for security. I feel pretty good about it, but you never know. Hopefully we will learn something from this Mohammed character."

Fortunately traffic was light due to the late night hour and they were soon turning into the dirt path leading through woods to the unprepossessing shack that buster had adapted and enlarged to serve the special needs required by CIA contract work.

As they walked up to the door Quint winked at Gerald, "Remember those pups I promised your boys? They are supposed to be delivered to your house today."

"If Jill doesn't kill you I'll be surprised." Gerald shook his head and laughed. "I don't think you should make a social call until I give you an all-clear."

"Aw, you know she loves me."

"Correction, she *likes you*. She *loves me*. And, even I wouldn't try to pull off that kind of surprise."

The humor vanished quickly when they arrived. Burke was standing on the porch waiting for them, his face grim. "I hate to tell you this, buddy, but it was a wasted trip. The guy just died of some kind of heart failure. Hollins tried to save him but there was nothing he could do. The man had lost too much blood. He was all pale and barely conscious when we got here and then he kind of passed out. He didn't come back to. We didn't get anything more out of him than what he told Quint at the Doc's office."

"Fuck." Gerald and Quint both swore under their breath at the same time. Gerald nodded his head to the interior. "Make him disappear. We'll give Doc a ride back to Washington while you clean up here."

Gerald and Quint entered the front area of the cabin where the Doctor was stowing his equipment in his bag. Buster had just made a cup of coffee. Holding it up, he asked, "Care for some."

"Yes. These late nights are killing me. I need a caffeine kick like a fish needs water." Gerald reached eagerly for the coffee.

"I'll take one, too. I didn't get my beauty sleep either," Quint responded.

Laughing while he winked at Gerald, Buster said, "Hell man, what makes you think sleep is going to make you pretty?"

"Vain wish. It obviously doesn't do much for your looks," Quint riposted.

Gerald laughed, "Hey, both of you sorry asses look handsome enough. Now, instead of trying to decide who's better looking, I need to pack it up and get back to Washington and see if we can stop this son-of-a-bitch before he does more damage."

Quint groaned, "Yeah, we should get there in just about time for morning traffic."

After thanking Buster for the use of the cabin, Gerald, Quint, and Hollins climbed into the black SUV for the drive back, leaving the others to take care of things deep in the Maryland woods. The three men rode in silence mile after mile, all lost in their own thoughts. Sitting in the back seat, Hollins watched the trees and buildings whiz by the window as the light changed from dark to the weak light of dawn. He commented to the back of Gerald's head, "Director, I'm sorry I couldn't save the guy because I know you wanted to get more information from him."

Gerald glanced over his shoulder, "Don't beat yourself up, Doc. We'll find another way to nail the bastard behind this shit."

Again they fell silent. Quint could only pray that Lila had been able to track the last message back to the originator. He knew it would not be easy. The proof of that was in the untraceable routing she had established for his computer. If she could do it, so could others. It was a constant struggle to stay one jump ahead of hackers. His mind mulled over the immediate problem. Stopping the plot against the lives of the President and Vice-President was a big problem. Unless they stopped him, the man or men behind it all would just keep trying to kill them. The immediate beneficiary of the plot was the very one that Gerald and Quint both suspected: the Speaker of the House, the successor should something happen to them. They were helpless to move against him until they had an airtight case. Forsyth was much too high up in Washington politics to be taken lightly. It was going to take a lot more than circumstantial evidence and suspicion.

"Fuck!" Gerald blasted the horn and swore as he swerved to avoid a pick-up truck that pulled into the slow moving traffic in front of him. Light rain had begun to fall making the morning DC traffic even more of a nightmare than usual. For the last few miles it had been bumper to bumper with road-idiots constantly lane changing only to get nowhere fast. "I think I'll resign and move to Figure Eight. I'm sick of driving in this traffic. And, I'm an idiot for not using the damned Agency chauffeur assigned to me. I just didn't want him to know the location of Buster's little hide away. Speaking of that, I have to ask you guys to keep it under your hats."

His voice heavy, Quint replied, "I already forgot where it is and I hope I don't have to go back. I would prefer to be at my beach house myself just kicking back on the sand getting a tan, but we won't either one quit until we nail this bastard. And, even if we nail him, there will always be others. As long as they are out there gunning for this country I don't see either of us quitting."

Gerald agreed, "That's certain. It just gets old. I can't help thinking about all those people who get up in the morning and go to work not worrying about anything but where to go for lunch."

Hollins commented, "Sorry, to disabuse you gents of the notion that the rest of us don't worry about anything but lunch. We all go to work with things on our minds, too. My problem is concern for the individual...who's sick, who's dying, those I can heal and those that I can't. Yours is more global, but that doesn't make me worry any less for my patients."

"I'm sorry Doc, no disrespect intended." Gerald continued, "You're right of course. Sometimes I think we have a tendency to get a little too self-important. I'm just disappointed as I really hoped we could discover who was pulling Mohammed's strings."

"I have mixed feelings. After what was done to my wife, I'm not sorry to see him dead. The only thing I regret is that he didn't die slower and a lot more painfully. I know any number of ways to accomplish that, as well as how to do it so no one is the wiser no matter what tests are run."

Quint laughed. "Jeez, Doc. You really do make me glad I'm not your patient."

Hollins didn't bother to respond.

Gerald was thoughtful for a minute, "Dr. Hollins, you have some skills that might come in very handy to the agency. Have you ever considered a little side practice?"

"In the future if there is anything I can do to nail bastards like these you can count me in." There was steel in his voice when he answered.

The addition of the doctor and Lila to Gerald's talent pool he considered a real positive. After the last few weeks of close contact with Quint he also realized that here was someone that had a far vaster range of abilities than anyone in the Agency had suspected. He would be thinking about how to best use those talents in the future now that many messages were no longer in code, but used simple language on social media that only those in the inner circle could interpret. If he could lure Lila from Raleigh and the job with the university, he would hire her in a minute. Tracking and infiltrating those networks was becoming increasingly critical and required an expanding pool of experts in computer networks and know-how.

Chapter 23

Teresa did not go to bed after cleaning up the broken shards of the champagne stem, rather she went to her small apartment and packed her most valued items into one bag. She did not know if she would ever be able to return for the larger items she cherished but could never carry. At three in the morning, she opened the door from her private sitting area that opened onto her own patio. Thankfully this end of the house was well screened by shrubs from both the chauffeur's quarters over the garage and the main house. With luggage in hand she walked all the way to the street on the edge of the lawn where shadows from the overhanging trees were deepest. She turned back once to stare at the dark and silent house before walking on. Even when she reached the street, she remained on the verge where she was hidden from any rare vehicle that might pass at such an early hour. She walked for more than three miles when she had no choice but to sit down on the suitcase while she struggled to catch her breath. She was getting too damned old for such shenanigans. But, there was no choice she told herself. Deep down in her gut, she knew something terrible had happened to Rena and that devil she had married was behind it. Somehow she must reach her sister's and recover those files. She intended to be standing at the gates of the CIA office when it opened. She did not know what was in the files, but it had to be important or Rena would not have guarded it so carefully and entrusted it to her. She pulled out the cell phone from her pocket, terrified that the light from the phone would reveal her if Forsyth had somehow awakened and followed. Hunching over the phone to conceal as much of the light as she could, she punched in the Uber number and asked for a pick-up. Now all she had to do was wait until the car arrived. She watched the driver's progress on the little I-phone screen while she prayed that she could do something for the sweet woman she had grown to love and pity with equal intensity. If Rena were to miraculously appear at home in the morning, she could only hope that she would be safe until someone could rescue her. Teresa prayed that was the case, and that turning over Rena's folder was the right thing to do. She didn't know what that devil of a husband was up to, but it had to be bad, really bad. Rena was frightened all the time and now she was as well.

Her sister clomped down the stairs in response to the repeated ringing of the doorbell, grumbling at who would be calling at the ungodly hour of four in the morning. She tugged the sash on the robe tighter when she reached the bottom. For a moment she was tempted not to open the door. Who knew who might be on the other side? Her quandary was interrupted by another insistent buzz of the bell followed by a voice she recognized as her sister's. Something was bad wrong for Teresa to be at her door in the wee hours.

Fumbling with haste, she unlocked the door and opened it. "For the love of God, Teresa, come in. You gave me a fright. What's going on to get you out in the middle of the night?"

"Rosa, I could be in a world of trouble and I don't want to get you all mixed up in the middle, but I've got nowhere else to turn."

"Come on in the kitchen and tell me about it while I make us some coffee."

When Rena had finished telling her the state of the Forsyth marriage and her suspicions, Rosa shook her head. "It is a huge mess for sure. What are you going to do about it?"

"I for sure ain't going back for the man to go messing with me. He don't know nothing about you so you should be safe. I'm going to take that file I gave you to the CIA office soon as it's open and tell them everything I know." Rena stopped to take a sip of her coffee. "I got this feeling way down in my gut that Douglas Forsyth has done something bad to that sweet wife of his and I don't know what all else he has done. She seemed to think that she had learned some serious stuff. She kept it in that folder she gave me to keep safe."

*****

Quint and Gerald had gone to his house after dropping off Hollins. Gerald went to bed to get a couple of hours of sleep accomplishing nothing but a lot of tossing and turning. Quint had no better luck on the sofa. He had already showered and was working at his computer when Gerald walked in still toweling his hair dry.

"Looks like you're up and working already. You got anything new?"

"There was an email from Lila. She thinks she's tracked the money. She's supposed to get back to us as soon as she can verify the total routing. According to what she's got so far, the money originated in Saudi Arabia and from there went to Credit Suisse and then to the Caymans. From the Caymans it landed at the Bank of America in Alexandria. The accounts at every bank are listed under different corporate names. She thinks they are shams set up to cover the ID's of the sender and receiver. Right now she's trying to trace the corporations."

"That's the best news I've heard in awhile. You be ready to leave for the office in fifteen? And keep it quiet as it is too early for the kids to be up."

"No problem. Any time you say."

He had just returned from lunch in the agency dining room when Gerald picked up his ringing phone. He listened without comment for several minutes before saying, "Yes, it does sound like the MO for the Hollins murder. I'm playing a hunch and I want you to keep my name out of it. How about giving a call to Congressman Forsyth and asking for a description of his wife? I am assuming he did not call you yet. You can say one of your officers thinks he recognizes her from an embassy function where he was moonlighting as a security guard. Record the conversation for me if you don't mind. Do a vaginal swab and send it to me by courier. I think I might have a lead on this for you. If I'm right, we need to sit tight. No press releases until we can figure out how to play it."

Quint walked into the office. "Hey Gerald, I just ran across this older lady wandering around in the foyer. She says she won't talk to anyone but you. Apparently they have shuffled her all over hell and back and she still refuses to leave. I have no clue what gives because she says she's not talking to the rest of us. Think you ought to see her?"

"Probably some crackpot. Do me a favor and find her. Tell her I sent you and that you need some information before she can pass clearance to see me. If she doesn't give you a damned good reason for hanging around, have security haul her ass out."

"On my way." Quint chuckled. He had spent a few minutes chatting with the woman and liked her. Her warmth reminded him of Mrs. Henderson. If she was legit, he had a job opening on Figure Eight. But, first he had to find out what had brought her to the CIA demanding to talk to the Director.

Quint found the woman in the lobby where she was again demanding the receptionist show her the way to the Director's office. With a voice that reflected the suffering and patience of Job, the receptionist intoned, "I have told you repeatedly, that the Director will not see people who do not have a prior appointment and some valid reason for the visit."

Quint watched the woman pull herself into a rigid five feet of outrage, "And I have told you that I have a serious reason for wanting to see him. I didn't truck all the way out here in an expensive taxi and waste my day standing around getting nowhere for no reason."

"Would you tell me what the reason is, at least?"

"I have told you folks over and over I ain't talking to nobody except the Director of this here CIA."

Quint hid his smile as he walked up to the irate woman. "Allow me to introduce myself. I'm Quinton Cord. The Director asked me to come down and chat with you a moment. Will you come with me, please?"

"How do I know the Director sent you to see me?"

Quint smiled, "I know you are aggravated with the bunch of us at the moment and I do apologize that we have not been more receptive. I can only ask you to trust me. Surely I don't look so very dishonest, now do I?"

"Hmph! A lot of people know how to put on the charm and they're nothing but rotten, evil stinkers underneath. My boss man is a first rate example of that."

"He's going to be upset you're not at work, isn't he?"

"No, he ain't. I done and quit that man. That's why I'm here."

Quint led her to a conference room, convinced she was totally batty. "Do have a seat. Could I get you some water or something?"

"You sure can! You can get me in to see the Director. I got to give him this here folder and then I need to find somewhere to lay low for a spell."

He thought he could detect fear in her voice as she looked around the stark conference room. Perhaps, she was having some kind of psychotic spell. He just hoped she was not dangerous. He decided he would be friendly, placate her, and persuade her to leave.

"I don't believe you gave me your name?"

"I'm Teresa Jones and my name don't mean no never mind around here. But, what I have in this folder might. So are you going to let me see this Director man?"

Forcing himself to remain patient, Quint said, "He cannot see you at the moment. That's why he sent me, Mrs. Jones."

"I ain't a Mrs. You just call me Teresa."

"I'll do that Teresa and I go by Quint with my friends." Quint leaned towards her, "Tell me what kind of work you do, Teresa?"

"I'm a cook and a housekeeper. I'm good at it, too, or I would've been fired by now for being friends with the boss's wife. He's mean and I'm afraid he's hurt her bad. She didn't come home last night and I ain't seen her in days. She gave me this folder and told me if anything ever happened to her to get it to someone that could use it to stop her husband from doing something bad."

"Do you know what she put in the folder?"

Teresa vigorously shook her head, "No, sir, I don't go snooping around in what ain't mine. Never have and I'm too old to start now."

"That is a fine trait to have." Quint leaned over and patted her hand, "If you would like to give me the folder I will see to it the Director gets it."

Teresa shook off his hand like he was a bothersome fly. "Ain't giving this folder but to one man and you ain't him."

Trying another tack, Quint asked, "Would you mind telling me the name of the wife you are so worried about? Maybe we can find her for you?"

"I'm scared it's too late to save her. I've told her over and over she had to get away from that man. I watched him hit her and treat her like dirt, keeping her shut away until he needed to pull her out to impress somebody. Something funny is going on with him and I don't mean funny ha-ha. A few days ago he acted real sweet like and talked her into meeting him at a hotel for this lovey-dovey get away. There ain't a thing lovey-dovey about that man. I ain't seen hide nor hair of her since she left."

"You haven't told me her name?"

"I'm scared to. That man is real important in this here town. If he knew I was here blabbing about him no telling what he would do to me."

"Teresa, I promise I won't let anything bad happen to you. Trust me, now."

She blew out her breath as she studied him, "You look alright to me. I guess there ain't much choice if I want to see the Director."

"That's right." He nodded encouragingly.

"I'll tell you, but you've got to protect me and I ain't kidding." She looked him in the eye as she said it, her voice stern.

"I promise."

She pursed her lips and studied him some more, "Alright. Her name is Rena Forsyth." She looked at him expectantly. "Does that ring a bell?"

Quint's eyes widened in shock, "My God, are you talking about Congressman Forsyth's wife?"

Her lips in a tight grim line, she nodded once.

"You just got an admission ticket to Director Williams' office. Let's go."

After hours of getting nowhere, the relief she felt was almost tangible. Her legs were shaking when she stood. There was no turning back now. She did not know what she had gotten herself into, but she was for sure in it.

Chapter 24

Gerald hung up the phone and turned to Quint, "The President is satisfied with the evidence we gave him. It is a ticklish situation politically as Forsyth is a powerful man and has long been a rival of the President's. You probably recall they were both vying for the nomination the last two elections."

"Yeah, I do. It's a pity Forsyth can't have a sudden heart attack, huh?"

"That is what the President wants me to talk to you about. Any ideas on how to do it? The President wants my hands clean in case there is an investigation. I don't want to throw you under the bus, as this would be a serious problem were anyone caught in an assassination plot against the Speaker."

"Wouldn't it just!" Quint sat for a moment thinking, "I've been reading about hacking into a car's electronic control system. It seems the steerage, throttle, and breaks can all be controlled remotely if you know how to break through the firewall. I can have Lila research it for me. If we could cause an accident that is untraceable back to us that would solve the problem. We just have to do it in such a way that no one else is hurt and it has to be fatal. After what he did to the Hendersons, I would love to strangle him with my bare hands, but that leaves evidence."

"There is the Prince to deal with as well."

"I speak Arabic and could probably get to him if you want me to handle it for you."

"I'm not sure. We are supposed to be allies with the Saudis.

Taking out a royal prince could be even more damaging that offing Forsyth."

Quint chuckled, "Why should we do the dirty work? We have enough on Fayed to tie him to the attacks in London and Paris that I can see any number of other interesting options. Not only that, but it seems to me that a discrete sharing of information with Saudi intelligence might discourage them from pursuing it with us.

"I like the way you think. I'll call Sidney and get it rolling in London and you call Lila and see what you can come up with."

*****

The morning following his wife's death, Douglas Forsyth was irritated. He had arisen to find a quiet house with no waiting coffee or breakfast. He had charged into Teresa's apartment without knocking intending to haul her lazy ass from bed if she was still sleeping. He didn't pay her good money to slack off on her duties just because his wife wasn't around. After checking her rooms, he was satisfied she had not left as her personal items were in evidence. But where in the hell was she? He damned well planned to chew her out when he saw her later.

Three days later, she still had not returned. He left the house furious at having to stop at Starbucks for coffee and a muffin. As if that were not enough, he spent the next two hours with the police. He had already been to the morgue and identified his wife. Now he sat through yet another grueling questioning session. It was a pity that her body had not been burned as he ordered and dumped in a more hidden location. That would have slowed the police down and given him time to find out if his wife had confided in the cook. As it was, he felt rather proud of the grieving husband act he had put on for police benefit. That and his powerful role in the government had been enough to assure a friendly an apologetic conclusion to the session.

For the next couple of days he planned a funeral for his late wife that would be worthy of someone married to a man of his station. As far as he was concerned, it was the ideal time to milk as much public sympathy as he could. It would stand him in good stead when it was time to run for office. Her body would not be released for several days more, so he had time to orchestrate appearances on the morning television newscasts. He thought it might be wise to hint that her death was retaliation against him for his recent criticism of the Republican policy against the Middle East. The morning news anchors would leap on the allegation and run with it. It amused him how much news one little remark based on unsubstantiated rumors could generate if dropped in the right quarters.

When his phone rang early the third morning after Rena's body was identified, he was expecting another call from CNN. He chuckled to himself. Apparently his appearance two days previous had boosted their ratings to the highest in years. He suspected they would want him back. Glancing at the screen he was disappointed when he recognized the number of the CIA. He had called it often enough he ought to know. A call from Director Williams was not what he needed at the moment, but after calling him to report his wife missing he didn't dare ignore it. After listening to the Director expressing sympathy for his wife's death, he nearly dropped the phone when he was told the CIA had two suspects in custody in a safe house in Maryland and while they were unconscious and in critical condition at the moment, the doctor suspected he could revive them at some point. His knuckles gripped the phone in terror. As a special courtesy, they were offering him the opportunity to be present at the interrogation. Fuck! He had no choice. If the two idiots spilled their guts they would ruin everything. Somehow he had to stop them before they talked. When he ended the call, Forsyth turned his car and headed for the address he was given in Maryland. He was determined to get there before Williams.

He had long since left the interstate and made several turns. The current road was two-lanes running through dense woods on both sides. In places the shoulders were crumbled. The paint in the centerline was worn to a ghostly white and the paint on the edges was not existent. The Maryland highway department appeared to have forgotten to maintain this one. He shook his head in disgust at the condition of the road when his tire hit yet another pothole. He had passed no one for at least twenty minutes and was making good time. Forsyth was only a few miles from his destination when he turned on the radio to see what the news was reporting about his wife's death. He listened to the usual speculations and the eyewitness description of the discovery of the body. It was pretty much boilerplate reporting. He smiled at the sympathy they expressed for her grieving husband, the "powerful congressman, Douglas Forsyth." The smile quickly vanished from his face at the next news item. "Royal Saudi Prince Fayed's naked body and that of a teenage boy have been found shot to death in his bed in Jeddah."

He had no time to deal with the shock as his car suddenly accelerated. Although he stomped the brake repeatedly the car continued to gain speed. He was struggling to control the speeding vehicle when the unexpected loss of power steering added to his woes. Sweating and swearing, he clung to a suddenly unresponsive steering wheel. He panicked at the sharp curve that loomed ahead and struggled even harder to gain control. Plunging off the road he screamed in horror as he stared at the huge oak directly in front of the car. He had been in the upper echelons of Washington power long enough to know the government was dealing with him in its own way.

*****

Quint held the morning newspaper as he nursed a cup of coffee. The lead story was a lengthy article about the death by vehicular suicide of Congressman Douglas Forsyth who was devastated by the murder of his beautiful wife. He suspected Forsyth would have loved the glowing details provided by the White House press describing the many accomplishments of the late Democratic powerbroker. Laying the paper to one side, he dropped a five-dollar bill on the table and walked out of the cafe just off Interstate 95. In just over an hour he would be on Figure Eight Island where Lila and Code were waiting for him.

Fiction Award
NC Society of Historians 2010

IIC Society of Historians
Established December 1941

AWARD WINNER

Judge's Comments:

"It feels like one is reading a living history rather than one fictitious by nature. The book is wonderfully written, and as the story unfolds, it is realistic in that it 'could' happen and probably did to many during the War Between the States, and it is exciting, heartbreaking, tense and relaxing.

Anybody interested in the War Between the States from a layman's view would enjoy reading this book. The story, which is difficult to chronicle in limited space, has been lovingly crafted by an author whose heart is in the South and whose soul is in her characters. Kudos for a job well-done. Kudos!"

Titles by Betty j. Vaughn

Title: *Yesterday's Magnolia*

- Paperback: 300 pages
- Language: English
- Hard Cover Book ISBN: 9781590955543
- Paper Back Book ISBN: 9781590955550
- eBook / ISBN: ISBN: 9781590955567

Jo envies Margo and Maurice for their ready charm, looks, wealth, glamour, and exciting lives never realizing that it is she who is envied for a life that contains the things that they themselves long for and have not attained.

"It's a shame to have so damned much and yet so little." An eastern North Carolina farmer's daughter, Margot, streaks like a comet into the life style of the rich and famous. Her beauty and exuberant, zestful personality gain her entrance to boardrooms, the White House, a corporate jet stocked with Cristal champagne and caviar, a villa in Italy, and marriage to one of the world's most powerful men. Maurice, the spurned suitor, seeks friendship and comfort from Margot's sister, Jo, a quiet, bookish art history teacher. Jo envies them both for their ready charm, looks, wealth, glamour, and exciting lives never realizing that it is she who is envied for a life that contains the things that they themselves have not attained. Like the comets they so resemble both Margot and Maurice are consumed by the friction of life, leaving Jo to remember the magic moments they brought to a more conventional path.

Title: *Tiger's Code*
- Paperback: 252 pages
- Language: English
- Hard Cover Book ISBN: 9781590953907
- Paper Back Book ISBN: 9781590953914
- eBook / ISBN: ISBN: 9781590953921

Quint Cord's latest assignment is proving to be his most challenging and could well lead to catastrophic events if he does not break the code in time to avert them.

Quint Cord is an unlikely spy. With sufficient family money so that he never needs to work, he could have spent his life idling on a beach chasing women. But from the moment he discovers famous codes of the past in a university class, he is hooked. His unique talent for creating and breaking codes brings him to the attention of the CIA.

A powerful and ambitious politician, who's in cahoots with a Saudi prince, plans to seize the US presidency and throw the western world into turmoil. Quint flees the country only to stay one step ahead of a foe determined to kill him before he can break the code.

Clue by clue, Quint begins to zero in on his target but can he stop him in time?

Title: *Run Cissy Run*

- Paperback: 300 pages
- Language: English
- Hard Cover Book ISBN: 9781590956748
- Paper Back Book ISBN: 9781590956755
- eBook / ISBN: ISBN: 9781590956762

You would think Cecilia LaRoque has it all: a loving father, wealth, beauty, social position and a devoted suitor. She doesn't. Crushed by a cold and critical mother who soon absconds to live with a dissolute lover, 'Cissy' struggles to prove herself worthy of love and respect. She could not have foreseen in her teenage years that the genteel and privileged life she had led would come to a crashing halt with the outbreak of Civil War, a bitter struggle that would tear her world apart. Despite the hardships and inherent danger, she seizes the opportunity to forge an unorthodox role for herself as a spy.

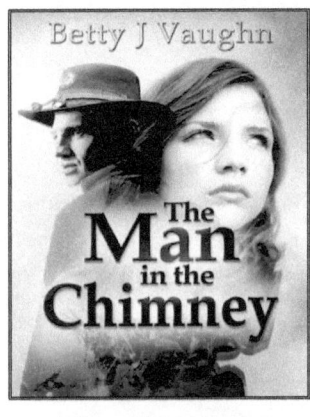

Title: *The Man In The Chimney*

- Paperback: 352 pages
- Language: English
- Hard Cover Book ISBN: 9781590956021
- Paper Back Book ISBN: 9781590956038
- eBook / ePub: ISBN: 9781590956045

The War Between the States has come to eastern North Carolina, bringing hardships, pillaging, and fear to the local residents. For those left at home, the struggle to procure the needs of daily life is all-consuming; for those serving in the armies of both North and South, death is a daily companion. Against this backdrop, an unlikely and forbidden love affair between a local woman and a Union officer leads to difficult choices for them both—choices that will tear them apart and force them to deal with the abandonment of their dream of a life together.

Despite broken hearts, misunderstandings, and missed chances, Penny and Ryan strive to survive the dangers and ravages of war and make the best of their separate futures. With the surrender of the South at Appomattox, Penny realizes she has one last chance to either find the man she loves or settle for a life alone.

Title: *Turbulent Waters*

- Paperback: 328 pages
- Language: English
- Hard Cover Book ISBN: 9781590951743
- Paper Back Book ISBN: 9781590951750
- eBook / ISBN: ISBN: 9781590951767

LOVE IS PERSONAL, WAR IS NOT, especially in North Carolina, 1865-1867, during the reconstruction. With a love they are certain will transcend all else, southern belle Penny Kennedy marries Union Officer and attorney, Ryan Madison, despite the condemnation of those around them. The initial days of wedded bliss end abruptly when Marcus, the man who courted Penny for years in anticipation that she would marry him, is arrested for murder, and Ryan is assigned to prosecute him. As hard as this development is to tolerate for Penny, she will discover worse things await her before Ryan and she can attain the life they desire.

Title: *The Intrepid Miss LaRoque*

- Paperback: 300 pages
- Language: English
- Hard Cover Book ISBN: 9781590957103
- Paper Back Book ISBN: 9781590957110
- eBook / ePub:: ISBN: 9781590957127

When Wilmington falls in February of 1865, Cissy LaRoque no longer needs to spy. That will not stop her from finding a new career where she can prove her worth beyond societal expectations of a woman. With the war drawing to an end and Wilmington occupied, she is faced with desperate circumstances. Ryan Madison, a Union officer from the past, and Brandon McLean, a new one, attempt to help her. While attracted to them both, she is aware of family and community hostility toward the enemy and dares not act on the attraction. Her fiancé, Logan who is fighting for the southern cause, does not arouse her ardor like the two Union men. When the Confederacy falls, she convinces her father to allow her to run his shipping office in New Berne while he maintains the main office in Wilmington. There she discovers Ryan has married and Logan has jilted her. Provoked and titillated by a man she cannot have but craves, she puts aside romance and concentrates on business. Despite her father's initial objections, much to his surprise she succeeds far beyond any expectation. Although she is happy in what she has achieved, she is frustrated by what she has lost.